MW00639181

Before We Forget Kindness

Also by Toshikazu Kawaguchi

Before the Coffee Gets Cold

Tales from the Cafe

Before Your Memory Fades

Before We Say Goodbye

Before We Forget Kindness

a novel

TOSHIKAZU KAWAGUCHI

Translated from Japanese by Geoffrey Trousselot

HANOVER
SQUARE
PRESS

Recycling programs for this product may not exist in your area.

ISBN-13: 978-1-335-91528-3

Before We Forget Kindness

First published in 2024 in the United Kingdom by Picador, an imprint of Pan Macmillan.
This edition published in 2024.

Originally published in Japan as やさしさを忘れぬうちに by Sunmark Publishing, Inc., Tokyo, Japan, in 2023.

Hanover Square Press
22 Adelaide St. West, 41st Floor
Toronto, Ontario M5H 4E3, Canada
HanoverSqPress.com

Printed in U.S.A.

contents

i

The Son

The café that could take you back in time was in Jimbo-cho, a district of the Kanda area in Chiyoda City, Tokyo. It was a little away from the nearest station, and its sign was placed outside in one corner of a quiet narrow alley-way.

The café's name was Funiculi Funicula. It was named after the popular Italian folk song from the Naples region, which had been commissioned to commemorate the opening of a cable-driven railway.

"Toward the fiery flames of Mt. Vesuvius
Let's go up the slope…"

That's what the Japanese lyrics say in this song, whose melody most people have heard at least once. Children in Japan recognize the melody as that of "The Imps' Pants," a Funiculi Funicula parody song. The reason why this time-traveling café was named after an Italian folk song was unknown, even to its owner.

The name of the owner, who always wore his cook's uniform, was Nagare Tokita. A towering figure more than two meters tall, Nagare was a quiet man with intense, almost threadlike narrow eyes. He was standing stoically with the composure of a powerful temple guardian statue. His wife, Kei Tokita, had worked at the café as a waitress. Always smiling with her big, bright eyes, she had been carefree and innocent, with a friendly and welcoming personality. Tragically, a heart-related illness claimed her life two years ago, leaving behind their daughter, Miki, who had big, bright eyes, just like her mother.

Kazu Tokita, the waitress, was Nagare's cousin. She had a fair complexion and narrow, almond-shaped eyes, with a straight nose and light-pink lips. Anyone would agree she was pretty if it was pointed out to them, but there was nothing that left a lasting impression. If they closed their eyes, they would struggle to remember what she looked like—she could be seen as both a young girl and a calm, mature woman. She was taciturn by nature and some customers said it was almost impossible to strike up a conversation with her.

A rumor was even floating around that she seemed to be without presence, like a ghost.

Presently, however, it was only Kazu who could pour the coffee that took you back in time.

Nagare shared the Tokita family name, but as a man, he was unable to pour the coffee. That ability was something only the women of the Tokita lineage possessed.

Often a customer would say, "Then please pour the coffee," as soon as they learned from Kazu they could go to the past if she did so.

But for that to happen…for a customer to be able to return to the past in this café, there were other annoying—as in extremely annoying—rules.

First and foremost: the Limited Time.

You see, the time you can spend in the past begins the moment Kazu has poured your coffee, and it ends just before the coffee gets cold.

Learning this tends to dismay everyone: "What? Is it really that short?"

What could anyone accomplish in the time it takes for one cup of coffee to get cold? You would have about ten minutes at most. Enough, perhaps, to eat a cup of instant noodles. It might take five minutes to boil the water, plus another three-minute wait after pouring it, leaving you just two minutes to eat. If you're having a night out, ten minutes would unlikely be enough time to receive any dish you ordered.

You would think that would dissuade everyone. But

no, some will say, "Oh well...but still, if I have a chance to go back to the past..."

Though on hearing the next rule, nearly all customers will conclude, "If that's the case, then I can't see any point in going back."

The reason they give up is the rule that nothing you do while in the past will change the present.

Regret comes in two flavors: actions taken and opportunities missed.

The regret from doing something stems from either not being able to undo it, or the awful outcome, such as hurting someone with an insensitive comment, or feeling wretched after declaring one's love.

The regret of not doing something, in contrast, relates to things left unsaid, or love never declared.

The most common reason for wanting to return to the past is to do something differently. But as nothing you do while in the past will change the present, anyone would just want to say, "Then what's the point of going back?"

Mind you, those aren't the only rules for going back to the past.

To make that journey, you must be sitting on a certain chair in the café. That chair, however, will be occupied by a certain other customer. And you will need to wait for that customer to vacate the chair to go to the toilet.

Now, if you are lucky, and you do get to sit in the

chair and go back in time, you must never get off it while in the past. Who you can go back to meet is also limited to people who have previously visited the café.

After hearing so many troublesome rules, some skeptical customers exclaim, "It seems like you're just hiding the truth that it's impossible to go back in time."

At times like these, rather than engaging in an argument, Kazu remains composed and responds, "If you say so." After all, the decision to go back to the past is ultimately up to each customer, and she finds it too tedious to argue.

Yuki Kiriyama was seven years old. He was carrying a shiny black-leather school bag on his back.

"Excuse me, may I ask you something?" Such polite and respectful phrasing was not normally heard from a child of that age.

The short-sleeved shirt of the prestigious private elementary school's uniform revealed his pale arms. His upright posture and taut spine bespoke a good upbringing. It was late June and too early for chirping cicadas, but outside was as hot as a midsummer day. In contrast to his composed expression, the sweat trickling down his face better encapsulated the childish charm of an elementary school student.

"Certainly, what is it?" responded Kazu Tokita. She had paused from her task and approached the boy. Whether she was conversing with adults or children, Kazu used the same manner of speaking.

"I heard a rumor that if I visit this café, I can go back to the past. Is that true?"

Without wiping away the sweat trickling down his face, Yuki looked up at Kazu.

Fumiko Kiyokawa, a café regular who had gone back in time three years earlier, couldn't help but interject, "You're an elementary school student, right? Where did you hear that rumor?" Her tone was very much how an adult would speak to a child. It sounded as if she was asking, *Surely you're not thinking of traveling back to the past?*

Never before had a boy come to the café wishing to do such a thing: if that really was why he had come, he would be the youngest to do so. But he would have to drink the entire cup of coffee poured for him by Kazu, and Fumiko thought an elementary school student was too young to be drinking coffee.

"When Mom and Dad were still living together, I heard tales of this café from my grandfather."

"Gosh."

Fumiko's expression darkened and she looked at Kazu. *Are his parents divorced?*

Kazu ignored this tacit inquiry, and without changing her complexion in the slightest, she replied, "Yes, you can go back."

Irreconcilable differences.

This is by far the most common reason for getting divorced nowadays. Other common reasons are financial difficulties, domestic violence, and infidelity. In a typical divorce, it would be reasonable to assume that several reasons are at play. Similarly, "irreconcilable differences" does not refer to a single reason for incompatibility: it's used to describe a combination of various unacceptable behaviors or persistent feelings of discontent that are difficult to move past or overcome in a relationship.

According to statistics, one or two people per thousand of the population are divorced in Japan. The hurdle for getting a divorce is lower now, so that is one reason.

Values are changing with regard to family and the community. These days, fewer families make the effort to introduce themselves to the people they live next to when they move in. In fact, it is not uncommon for residents of apartment buildings in urban areas not to even know their neighbors' faces.

Also, with the popularity of smartphones and webcams, we can now communicate face-to-face with friends and loved ones, even far away. As a result, people can manage perfectly well without building new relationships in their neighborhood or on their block, and that might be one reason for the growing number of nuclear families. However, the nuclear unit is being broken up further, and nowadays emphasis is placed more on the individual. In fact, this is a growing trend within the household, and husbands and wives are more and more often living as individuals.

Much of the stress people experience in their lives arises from their relationships with those immediately around them, such as a mother or father, child, sibling, friend, colleague, or, of course, spouse.

When two individuals who have been living their own lives based on their unique lifestyles and routines get married and start cohabiting, they will inevitably spend a significant amount of time together, sharing their lives.

Of course, since both partners have recognized each other as lifetime companions and begun married life together, it becomes necessary to adjust their lifestyles and routines to better accommodate each other. As long as love exists between them, these adjustments can be viewed as a source of happiness and freshness in their relationship. But if the love begins to fade and emphasis is placed on individualism, problems may arise and things that were tolerated due to love may become unbearable, and that kind of breakdown is not necessarily due to easily identifiable reasons such as money, domestic violence, or infidelity.

Things that were forgivable among friends may become intolerable later on. Such a turning point could be when the relationship evolves into a romantic one, when the couple begin living together, or when they get married.

Irreconcilable differences cannot be boiled down to clear reasons. Things just don't seem to work out, and the situation becomes unbearable and uncomfortable. Despite this, it's not that the parties involved hate each other.

If only we weren't married, we could get along just fine.

The idea of returning to an earlier, more amicable relationship is seen as one way to escape the tension of always walking on eggshells.

We got on better before we were married. Let's return to that.

There seems to be only one option to alleviate the stress and avoid disliking one's family.

Let's start anew and give ourselves a second chance.

And divorce is chosen.

That is, of course, only one example and not applicable to all couples who divorce.

But there was a boy who, caught in the middle of a crisis of individualism between his parents, agonized over the situation.

Yuki was regretting the time he had burst into tears at this café.

It all started at breakfast on Christmas morning last year. Out of the blue, his father, Kenji, suggested, "Yuki, how about we go to Disneyland?"

Yuki was confused: Kenji often claimed to be busy with work, and was seldom at home.

"Don't you have work?"

"What? Don't you like the idea?"

"No. It's not that."

Yuki glanced across the table at his mother, Aoi, who was eating toast. Whenever Aoi consulted with Kenji, he would always say, "I'm busy with work, so I'll leave the household matters to you," so Yuki thought he should check with his mother before replying to his father's invitation.

"That sounds like a nice thing to do. It's Christmas, after all, right?" Aoi said.

"Absolutely," Kenji agreed.

It had been a while since Yuki had seen Aoi smiling in front of Kenji, so he exclaimed with joy, "All right, let's go!"

They headed to Disneyland by car. Aoi drove, with Yuki in the front passenger's seat. It was smooth driving at first, taking just under twenty minutes from their home in Kanda, central Tokyo, via the Metropolitan Expressway Route 4 to the Kasai Interchange, their planned exit on the Bayshore Route. Being Christmas, however, it was heavily congested.

"I told you we should have exited at Urayasu Interchange."

"Well, you should have driven, then."

"What? You offered to drive."

"Only because you said you wanted to do some work in the car. You've got a nerve back-seat driving now."

Kenji and Aoi had been bickering like this since they left home, and that day was no different from most days. The two had begun to quarrel over trivial matters a few years ago: the cause was their different values and beliefs about work and parenting.

After Yuki was born, Aoi was thinking that she could put him in childcare and return to her job at an advertising agency. However, Kenji insisted, "I want you to devote your energies to being a mom for Yuki, because his early years until he turns three will have a huge impact on shaping his personality."

"Yes, that's a good point. All right, I think I can endure putting my career on hold until Yuki turns three," said Aoi, understanding Kenji's perspective.

Kenji made no reply, but he didn't like Aoi's word "endure." *Why does she make it sound like I'm asking too much? Shouldn't a mother's first instinct be to prioritize her child?*

There was nothing negative about Aoi's thoughts. She was simply expressing how she would have to endure a wait before she could return to the job she loved. Although she was actually thinking, *Raising Yuki is far more important to me than my work*, she did not convey that to Kenji.

Since that conversation, Kenji said, "I'll leave the household matters to you," about everything they discussed. Subconsciously embedded in his answer was his belief that Motherhood is a full-time job.

This rubbed Aoi the wrong way. *Why do you push me so hard to concentrate all my time on Yuki? You just seem to avoid your responsibilities as a father by using your work as an excuse. But if I say anything, we will just end up quarreling.*

Just as Kenji felt dissatisfaction with her, Aoi was suppressing her resentment toward him. She quietly kept her feelings bottled up until Yuki was three, but then she found herself so occupied with looking after him that her desire to resume her career gradually diminished.

"Weren't you planning to go back to the agency?"

"Well, perhaps if you helped more with Yuki and the housework."

"I don't have time for that. You know how busy I am. I'm even having to work at weekends."

"If I start working again, it'll be the same for me. Then who will take care of Yuki?"

"We can put him in childcare."

"Don't say it so casually."

"What do you mean? We agreed from the beginning that it would be until Yuki turns three."

"You were the one who said that, weren't you?"

"Didn't you agree, though?"

"So, what are you saying? You want me to balance work and household chores?"

"You said you wanted to return to work knowing that."

"That was three years ago. I didn't know raising a child would be this hard, and also…"

"What?"

"I didn't expect you to be this uninterested in child-rearing."

"It's not that I'm uninterested. I've been working hard to support our family. Now it's your turn to return to work and give me a break."

"What? You make it sound like I've been playing around for the past three years."

"Oh, come on. Looking after a kid is a bit different from work."

"Then I think you should try it yourself. You'll see how difficult it is."

"But how can I do that? I'm working."

Their bickering was a tit-for-tat exchange fueled by intense emotions, and as a result, what they truly meant was distorted, and they were not understanding each other.

By the time Yuki was old enough to understand what was happening around him, his parents were quarreling every day, and he always stepped in to mediate.

Even in the car on the way to Disneyland that Christmas morning, he interjected, "I wish I could have taken over the driving. Sorry, Mom." Yuki's words were not a lie: he earnestly wished he could have changed places and driven. Aoi fully understood his sentiment, and Kenji was proud of his son's unparalleled kindness.

"It's okay, Yuki. It was Mom and Dad's fault. Today is Disneyland, so let's be nice to each other. Right, Dad?" Aoi looked intently at Kenji in the rearview mirror.

"Oh, right." Kenji's expression changed as if he had just remembered something. He closed his laptop and stowed it away in his bag.

"Sorry, Yuki. Dad won't be doing any more work today." Kenji bowed his head apologetically to Yuki from the back seat.

"Okay," replied Yuki, revealing a big smile.

Since they arrived at Disneyland late, they had to park some distance away. Then at the park entry gates, after passing through baggage inspection, they joined the end of a long queue to the ticket counter. By now, two and a half hours had passed since they left home.

Disneyland sometimes imposes entry restrictions at weekends, holidays, and Christmas Day. Even when they were finally able to enter the park, they would have to wait several more hours to ride the popular attractions.

Some time ago, there was an urban legend: couples who go to Disneyland break up. Perhaps it was mischievously spread by rival amusement parks, but if there was some sliver of truth to this statement, it most surely would be due to the long waiting times.

Waiting times were much longer before the introduction of the Standby Pass, sometimes exceeding an hour and a half. If a couple who owned annual passes had a favorite attraction or one in mind they wanted to ride, the waiting time would not be so bad. However, for couples who weren't avid fans of Disneyland and didn't possess one, the wait could be far longer than expected, exhausting conversation topics and leading to awkward silences, or even quarrels. Then, as tales of couples splitting up after going to Disneyland accumulated, an urban legend was born.

Whether or not Yuki had ever heard of it, his reasons for wanting to go to Disneyland were different. For there are also lucky superstitions attached to Disneyland, such as If you go, you will become happy. For example, If you hold hands with Mickey or Minnie, you will find love and If you go to Disneyland, you will conceive a child. Such lucky superstitions are groundless. But as Disneyland is known as the kingdom of dreams, it's the perfect place for visitors seeking happiness through good-luck omens. One lucky superstition is that If you make a wish at the last gate of "It's a Small World," it will come true.

"It's a Small World" is an attraction that takes visitors around the countries of the world on a gondola floating on water. Yuki was planning to make a wish at that gate.

Fortunately, after their argument in the car, Kenji and Aoi never lost their smiles during the long wait. They were only able to experience one popular attraction, but Yuki felt satisfied: he had been able to make a wish as their gondola passed the last gate in "It's a Small World."

Kenji drove them home. Yuki slept in the back seat, his head in Aoi's lap. For the first time in years, all three members of the family had spent a holiday together. Yuki was exhausted from the pure excitement of that alone.

"Yuki, we've arrived. Wake up," said Aoi.

The destination ended up being a café located close to their home.

They had parked in front of Jimbocho Station with the plan of eating dinner, but it was Christmas Day and all the restaurants were fully booked. Heading away from the station, they walked down a quiet alleyway where they found a café sign. Kenji went inside to see if there was a table. In spite of its being Christmas, there was just one customer. The waitress told him that they also served light meals and cakes.

Yuki was thrilled that the three of them could celebrate Christmas in a way that was very Christmaslike.

When Kenji had popped in, each of the tables had only two chairs, but the taciturn waitress Kazu Tokita had already prepared a chair for Yuki.

"Hello. Welcome. What would you like to drink?"

"We came by car, so I'll have a non-alcoholic beer. My wife will have a glass of champagne and an orange juice for my son."

"Coming right up," called out Nagare Tokita, wearing his cook's uniform. Nestled in his arms was a little girl of about two years old with big round eyes. Her name was Miki. Nagare was so big, he made Miki look as small as a squirrel as she snuggled up against his chest.

There was a decorated Christmas tree in the café, but no Christmas songs were playing. All that could be heard was a soft, spell-like mumbling of "Jingle bells, jingle bells" from Miki in the kitchen.

A Christmas evening without music would surely feel unsatisfying and strange for the ordinary customer, but neither Kenji nor Aoi seemed bothered. The three of them were enjoying reminiscing over their day at Disneyland while eating the meal Kazu had quietly brought them.

Although it was Christmas night, no more customers came. The only other customer was the woman in the very unwintry, short-sleeved white dress seated in the furthest corner of the café.

It was truly an intimate moment between a child and his parents. For Yuki, it was supposed to be a memorable happy time that he hadn't experienced in years. But a sad reality was waiting for him.

When Yuki took the first bite of Christmas cake, Kenji spoke up.

"Yuki."

"What?"

A big thing about Christmas is the presents. But that was far from Yuki's mind. Spending the day with his family at Disneyland and then eating delicious food and Christmas cake were the greatest gifts for him. Even at the last gate of "It's a Small World," he didn't want any of the games or toys that an ordinary elementary school student might want.

Yuki felt that this was the happiest time of his life.

Dong

One of the large clocks in the coffee shop struck its bell, indicating that it was 7:30 p.m. Aoi reached out and placed her hand on Yuki's small head.

"We have something important to say, Yuki. Your father and I have decided not to live together anymore."

"What?"

"Tonight will be the last night the three of us spend together," Kenji added.

Yuki's mind went blank upon hearing Aoi and Kenji's sudden confession.

The last Christmas.

All Yuki remembered was that his crying had upset Kenji and made Aoi cry, and hearing Miki singing the full chorus of "Jingle Bells" from the back of the kitchen. He couldn't remember how he got home.

However, he could never forget the next morning when he woke up. He saw two gift boxes placed next to his pillow, and he cried silently.

"You know," Fumiko said, after listening to Yuki's story with teary eyes, "I really understand how you feel. I do. But how should I put it… Even if you go back to the past, you know about the rules, right?"

Fumiko turned to Kazu, who was listening to the

conversation, and appealed to her for support. Fumiko believed that Yuki was attempting to travel back in time to prevent his parents' divorce. She knew that there was a cruel rule operating in this café that would shatter the young boy's innocent wish.

I wonder if he'll cry again when he learns about the rule.

As Fumiko was hesitating, Kazu stepped in front of Yuki and without changing her expression told him, "If you go back to the past, there is nothing you can do that will change the reality of your father and mother separating."

What?! He's only seven! You could have sugarcoated it a bit!

Contrary to Fumiko's expectations, however, Kazu's explanation did not upset Yuki. Instead, he replied with a determined look in his eyes that seemed beyond his years, "Yes, that's all right."

"Eh? So why do you want to go back to the past?"

Fumiko leaned forward, studying Yuki's expression.

"I shouldn't have cried that day."

"What do you mean?"

There was more to Yuki's story.

Since the day at Disneyland, Yuki had been living with his mother. His parents' divorce was finalized after the new year. Yuki thought that he would continue to live with Aoi.

One day, Aoi mentioned to Yuki that there was someone she wanted him to meet, so they planned a dinner at a city restaurant. When they arrived, they were greeted by a man who seemed older than Kenji. He had a kind demeanor and an average build.

"Good evening, Yuki. Nice to meet you. My name is Makoto Nishigaki."

As Nishigaki removed his coat, he bowed politely to Yuki, standing next to Aoi.

"Good evening. I'm Yuki Kiriyama. Nice to meet you."

Yuki returned the greeting just as politely, drawing a nod of approval from Nishigaki.

"You're quite well-mannered when it comes to greetings. That's impressive. I'm sure you'll accomplish great things in the future."

"Thank you."

A waiter showed them to their table. The meal went smoothly. Yuki's eyes sparkled when he heard about Nishigaki catching a giant trevally weighing over thirty kilograms while fishing in Okinawa and Miyako Island.

"I'll take you with me next time."

"Really?"

"Yes, I promise."

"Yay!" Yuki exclaimed spontaneously.

"Actually, Yuki," interjected Aoi, who had been quietly listening to the conversation, "your mom is dating Mr. Nishigaki."

Nishigaki straightened his back in response to Aoi's announcement. Yuki, unable to fully grasp the meaning of what she had said, looked back and forth between them.

"Does that mean...?" First, Yuki's mind conjured the image of his father. In his imagination, Kenji, standing next to Aoi, was replaced by Nishigaki. He voiced the conclusion he drew from there. "You are getting married?"

"Well, we want to live together."

In Yuki's mind, he, Aoi, and Nishigaki entered a single house, while Kenji was left standing alone outside.

"What will happen to Dad?"

"About that..." Aoi proceeded to inform Yuki. The reasons Kenji and Aoi separated was not only because their personalities clashed, but also because they each had someone else they were interested in. After talking it over thoroughly, they decided to part ways for their own sakes. However, they both wanted to live with Yuki, so, after living with his new father for a month, they wanted him to live with his new mother for a month. After that, he should decide whether to live with Kenji or Aoi.

"Okay, I understand," said Yuki, agreeing to spend a month living with Aoi and Nishigaki.

The following day, it was arranged that Yuki would meet Kenji's partner, a woman he didn't know. It was a Sunday, and Kenji picked him up in his new car. They headed to a small cake shop, where all sorts of colorful cakes were displayed in the window. Kenji introduced Yuki to the woman who made them, explaining that she was his current girlfriend.

Her name was Kaede Kimura. She was a head shorter than Aoi, and though she was the same age as Kenji, she still radiated the youthfulness of a teenager. Kenji laughed, saying that if Yuki walked with her, they might be mistaken for siblings.

"Who said you shouldn't have cried? Your father and mother put their own convenience before your feelings. It's natural for you to cry. You're not in the wrong. Why do you have to regret crying?" Fumiko said crossly. Her eyes were red and teary after listening to Yuki's story.

"Thank you, miss," Yuki said, smiling at the tearful Fumiko. "But I made a wish at Disneyland. I wished that my father and mother would be happy."

"What?"

"After I lived with Mr. Nishigaki and then with Kaede, I realized something."

"And what was that?" Fumiko's furrowed brow revealed her intrigue.

"When Mom was with Mr. Nishigaki, she was always smiling. It was the same with Dad, too. When he ate dinner with Kaede, he was always in a good mood, saying how delicious everything was. That's when I realized the wish I made at Disneyland had come true. So, I want to redo that day. Both Dad and Mom ended up being happy, so rather than crying, I want to give them a smile."

"But, still..."

Unable to accept Yuki's reasoning, Fumiko was frowning. But she couldn't express her objections. She had no right to deny Yuki's decision.

"So please let me go back. I want to return to Christmas last year—the day I ended up crying," said Yuki, bowing his head to Kazu.

"All right then."

"Kazu, seriously?" reacted Fumiko, casting a doubtful glance at Kazu as she spoke. "I know it is not my place to object. But I can't stay quiet on this. Why does such a young child have to go through all this for the convenience of the grown-ups? I simply fail to see how sending this boy back to the past could lead to his happiness! If his parents were to hear his words now, maybe they'd even..." and as Fumiko looked into Yuki's eyes, she kept the words that were to follow—*consider rethinking the divorce*—from leaving her lips.

I'm just saying what I think is right, not what the boy is hoping for.

Rather than something for himself, Yuki was wishing for his parents' happiness. On seeing such pureness of purpose in the boy's eyes, Fumiko realized it was she who was mistaken.

In this world, there are countless situations where sound reasoning doesn't necessarily lead to the right answer. Biting her lip, Fumiko took a couple of steps back and limply leaned against the counter stool.

Flap.

Echoing through the quiet café was the sound of a book being closed by the woman in the white dress, who was sitting in the seat that allowed you to travel back in time.

"Ah!" exclaimed Fumiko.

Everything is ready for him to travel back in time. How can I stop it now when it's not my place to object?

Fumiko's eyes followed the woman in the white dress as she silently passed in front of her.

"Come on. You can sit down now."

Kazu was guiding Yuki to the seat where he could

travel back in time. Once seated, Yuki gave Fumiko a warm smile. A surge of emotion welled up within her.

It's really none of my business, but do his parents know this side of him? I really want to show them!

Fumiko wishfully clasped her hands in front of her chest. It wasn't long before Kazu returned from the kitchen carrying a silver kettle and a pure white coffee cup on a tray.

"Do you know the rules?"

"I think so. But could you tell me them, just in case?"

Fumiko nodded vigorously. She was not doubting him, but better safe than sorry.

One by one, Kazu carefully explained the rules, which she must have explained dozens, if not hundreds, of times before. To each one, Yuki responded, "I understand. That's fine," but to the rule that the coffee must be drunk before it gets cold, he replied more solemnly. "Drink the coffee before it gets cold… Drink it before it gets cold… Before it gets cold."

"Are you ready?"

"Yes."

Everything was prepared. Kazu just needed to pour the coffee into the cup and Yuki would be able to travel back in time.

"Okay, then," said Kazu as she reached for the silver kettle.

"Ah! Wait a moment!"

Fumiko suddenly raised her voice. Kazu was unperturbed, however, and with her hand still on the kettle, she turned to Fumiko and waited for her next words.

"Kazu, shouldn't you put that thingamabob in the cup? You know...the alarm." Fumiko was making a pinching gesture with her fingers.

The café had a device that would sound an alarm to notify the person during their trip to the past when the coffee was about to cool completely.

Fumiko was suggesting that it be set for the seven-year-old Yuki. But Kazu simply replied, "I'm sure it will be fine," and turned her gaze to Yuki.

"But..."

Before Fumiko could attempt to stall the process once again, Kazu whispered, "Before the coffee gets cold." She lifted the silver kettle and tipped it toward the cup placed in front of Yuki.

A single wisp of steam rose from the filled coffee cup, and at the same time, Yuki's body also transformed into a steamy vapor.

Why?

With a lingering uneasiness in her heart, Fumiko watched as Yuki vaporized and was sucked up into the ceiling.

I used to love seeing Mom and Dad smile. They smiled best when they were together. When both were smiling, I couldn't help but smile with them.

My parents don't believe me, but I remember seeing their faces the moment I opened my eyes after I was born. Dad was looking at me hesitantly, leaning in to get a closer look at me, while Mom kissed my cheek and pressed her forehead against mine. I also remember Mom smelling nice.

The first word I ever said was "mama." It was just a word that came out while I was trying to communicate that I was hungry, but I soon realized that every time I said it, Mom was delighted. So I kept saying "mama" just because I wanted to see her happy face.

But it only had that effect on Mom. Dad would look sad for some reason and respond with "papa, papa." Later, when I caught on that "mama" meant "mother" and "papa" meant "father," I felt terrible that I might have hurt Dad's feelings. Sorry, Dad.

I have so many happy memories with Mom and Dad. They celebrated when my teeth came through, and they hugged each other and rejoiced when I took my first steps. If Mom and Dad smiled, then I was happy, too.

Also, I don't think Dad knows, but Mom put her heart and soul into cooking to make him happy. When Dad ate her meals and declared them "tasty," Mom would smile so beautifully. Dad's "tasty" was a source of happiness for Mom. That I am sure of.

There are things Mom doesn't know, too. When Dad came home late from work and Mom was already asleep, he would always kiss her forehead. Then when he saw that I was watching, he would say, "This is our secret!" Dad really loved Mom.

It was from a TV show that I learned the rumor that if you made a wish at the final gate of "It's a Small World" it would come true, and I decided that if I ever went to Disneyland, I would wish for Mom and Dad to be happy.

But eventually, Dad's work became busier. Mom said she couldn't go back to work because of me and started quarreling with Dad. I told Mom over and over again, "Mom, I'm old enough to be left at home alone now," but she only looked sad.

Guessing it was because I was still a child, I decided I had to grow up. So, I tried my best to become independent and do everything on my own. I wanted to quickly become a grown-up to help Dad with his work and make it so that Mom didn't have to worry about me. That way, they would surely smile like they used to.

That's what I thought.

But it wasn't the case. This wasn't the only place where Mom and Dad could find happiness. There were other places where they could smile.

I'm happy for them. I really am.

"When did you sit over there?"

Hearing Kenji's baffled question, Yuki opened his eyes. "Ah, um…"

Indeed, last Christmas, they had sat as a family at the table for two in the middle of the café. He remembered a chair had been added.

On the other side of the table, receiving both Yuki's and Kenji's gaze, Aoi was studying Yuki with a puzzled expression.

"Well, never mind. Hey, we're going to have cake soon, so come back and sit with us."

Kenji did not probe into Yuki's change of seat, as sudden as if he had teleported. It should have been impossible. But Kenji's non-reaction was due to the mysterious power of the café. At work here was the same force that ensured that no matter how much one tries while back in the past, the reality of one's original time will not change.

This power made the café's unsuspecting patrons simply accept anyone suddenly appearing in that particular seat with a "What? Oh, I guess that's fine." The reason was simple: if everyone was preoccupied by the weirdness of the situation, the coffee would get cold before any meaningful time could be had.

Yuki felt relieved that Kenji did not pursue it, but despite having been told to return to the family table, he was constrained by the rule that he couldn't move from the seat he was sitting in. If he did, he would be pulled back to his original time. He didn't expect this might happen, so while unable to stand up, he couldn't think what to do next.

Just then, Nagare Tokita emerged from the kitchen and said, "Since the table is quite cramped, would you like me to serve the cake over here?"

Kenji and Aoi exchanged glances and then looked at their table. Since they had meals for three on a table meant for two, it was indeed crowded with no space for the cake. They could wait for the table to be cleared, but as the owner said it was fine to change seats, it would be quicker that way. Agreeing to Nagare's suggestion, they moved to the other table.

"Thank you," said Yuki to Nagare, who replied, "You're welcome." His facial expression suggested that he had understood the situation and simply done the obvious.

Yuki was also seated at a table meant for two, so Kenji brought his own chair. Aoi sat across from Yuki, with Kenji in between them.

As Aoi sat down, she noticed the coffee in front of Yuki and reached for the cup, saying, "Excuse me, could you please take this away?"

"No, it's fine. This is my coffee." Yuki quickly clung on to the cup, causing Kenji and Aoi to exchange glances.

"You can't drink coffee, can you?"

"That's right. What's got into you?"

Yuki hastily made up an excuse to satisfy his parents' suspicions. "Today is a day that I have to become a grown-up. So, I'm drinking coffee."

On hearing his words, the two averted their gazes awkwardly.

"But don't force yourself to drink it. If you can't, Mom will drink it for you," Aoi said with concern.

"If you like, please use this," said Kazu Tokita, placing a small jug beside Yuki's cup. It was filled with milk. Normally, adding milk and sugar to coffee would make it easier to drink. This, however, was not a normal cup of coffee. Yuki stared at the jug, worried that the coffee would cool down the instant he added the milk. Kazu quickly added, "Don't worry. No matter how much you add, it won't affect the coffee's temperature."

Kenji and Aoi tilted their heads in confusion; Yuki alone understood Kazu's words.

"Thank you," he said, with a polite bow of the head.

Nothing, not just milk, will cause a change. Even attempting to heat the cup will not change the temperature of the coffee. Just like the rule that the reality of your original time cannot change no matter what you do in the past, the temperature of the coffee cannot be artificially manipulated no matter how hard you try. Here, too, the mysterious power of the café is at work.

"Sorry for the wait."

As Yuki poured milk into his cup, stirring in sugar as well, Nagare came out of the kitchen carrying a Christmas cake. On the cake was a plaque with "Merry Christmas" written in white chocolate.

On this Christmas night last year, just as Yuki had put a forkful of cake in his mouth, a pendulum wall clock chimed. Then Aoi, while stroking Yuki's head, had started a conversation with, "We have something important to say, Yuki."

He still remembered the warmth of her hand. As he recalled how he had burst into tears last Christmas, he thought to himself:

Even though Mom and Dad are separating, they will become happy with Kaede and Mr. Nishigaki. So, I should just smile, say, "I understand," and drink the coffee.

Aoi had cut and served him a slice of cake; the setup was now complete. All he needed to do was to take a bite.

However, no amount of time could pass that would bring Yuki to stick his fork into the cake.

"Huh?"

"What's the matter?"

Aoi peered into Yuki's face. His hand remained poised, motionless, while the chime of the clock's bell rang throughout the café.

Dong

Kenji studied Yuki's expression.

"Hey, Yuki, why are you crying?"

"What?" Yuki dropped his fork and brought his hands up to his face. "No way."

His cheeks were indeed wet. Tears were running down his cheeks.

"I'm not crying. I'm not crying."

Yuki tried desperately to wipe away his runaway tears but he couldn't stop them. It made Aoi cry, too. Wiping his tears with her finger, she asked, "What's made you so sad?"

Kenji stared intently at the slice of cake with a conflicted expression.

Yuki continued to cry in a voice that echoed throughout the café. It was even louder than when he had cried last Christmas.

Miki's rendition of "Jingle Bells" could be heard from the kitchen.

Repeating, "I'm sorry, I'm sorry," Yuki finished his coffee.

"Please move."

At the voice of the woman in the white dress, Yuki realized he had returned to the present. After hurriedly switching seats, he sobbed, "I cried again."

Fumiko gave the distraught Yuki a gentle hug.

"Not to worry. No one said you mustn't. Things are hard when your parents split up. It's okay to cry."

Yuki's sobbing grew even louder.

It was unclear whether the past Kenji and Aoi had spoken about their divorce in front of the weeping Yuki. Perhaps, because he cried, they couldn't mention it that day. But the present cannot change. At some point, the two of them would tell him about their decision to part. The rule of this café would prevail.

Later, after crying his last tear, Yuki fell asleep.

"That boy truly cares for his parents."

Kozo Morita, Aoi's father, had come to pick Yuki up. Morita lived by himself in an apartment not that far from the café. His wife had passed away two years earlier and he was looking after Yuki while he decided whether to live with Kenji or with Aoi.

"I was the one who told him about this café."

"Is that so?" responded Kazu from behind the counter.

"Even though he is only seven years old, he's been constantly worried about my daughter and Kenji. He's been regretting that he cried here last year. Seeing him stoically cope like this, I suggested he try returning to that day, but..." Morita glanced sadly behind at the sleeping Yuki he was carrying on piggyback.

"If I may ask..." Fumiko, who had stood up to see them off, called to Morita as he headed toward the exit. "Has he already decided who he wants to live with?"

"You seem concerned?"

"Yes. He seems so kind and conscientious. I'm sure he must be conflicted over having to choose between his father and mother."

In reaction to her words, Morita pressed down on the inner corner of his eye.

"He's been struggling with that decision for a while. And I'm sure he is still in a dilemma. I felt like scolding my daughter for getting a divorce despite knowing how he was feeling. But if I had said anything, it would have only upset him. I don't want to see him sad." Morita sniffed once.

"It's admirable that he is selflessly considering his parents. But the dear boy is only seven. I know he wanted to go back and show a big smile. But when he returned crying, I honestly thought it was for the best."

"Yes, I think so, too," Fumiko agreed, and at her words, Morita revealed a faint smile and left the café with a bow.

CLANG-DONG

Coming back into the café after seeing off Morita carrying Yuki on his back, Fumiko let out a big sigh.

"Is something wrong?" Kazu asked.

It was unusual for her to make such an inquiry, as she tended to avoid interacting with people. Then again, three years after Fumiko had traveled to the past, she had been coming to the café on almost a daily basis, whenever her schedule allowed. So Kazu had grown to feel less uncomfortable with her. Not that Fumiko was one to notice such a subtle diminishment of emotional distance.

Fumiko sat at the counter.

"If I had such a sweet, kindhearted son, and he burst into tears before me, I can't fathom how I could divorce…"

"I see."

"What would you do in that situation, Kazu? Would you still divorce?"

"I, er…" Kazu muttered. She glanced over at the

woman in the white dress. "I don't have the right to be happy."

"What? Why would you...?"

CLANG-DONG

Just as Fumiko tried to delve into Kazu's cryptic statement, the bell rang, and Nagare entered with Miki in one arm. He was carrying a bag full of groceries.

"We're back," announced Miki.

"Oh, er, welcome," replied Fumiko, partly distracted by Kazu disappearing into the kitchen.

"Hey, Fumiko! Don't you have work?"

"Miki, it's rude to speak like that," Nagare said sternly to Miki's obnoxious words.

"Oh, Nagare, it's fine. I'm used to it by now."

"Sorry. She just parrots everything she hears on the TV."

"Ah, voilà! I am a true Parisienne, non?"

"You don't really understand what that means, do you?"

"What do you mean, cherie?"

"That's enough!"

"Fumiko, get to work, s'il vous plaît."

"Hey!" retorted Nagare.

Fumiko burst out laughing at the exchange between the two.

"I'm sorry, Fumiko. Hey, Miki, isn't *Bean Bun Man* starting soon? Why don't you go out the back and watch TV?"

"Okay. See you later, Fumiko."

"See you later, Miki."

"I'm Germ Man! Ha He Hi Ho Hu!" exclaimed Miki as she left Nagare's arm and ran off to the back room, where there was a living space.

"I am really sorry, Fumiko."

"Oh, it's nothing. Isn't it great that she is so full of energy? Miki has a brightness that neither you nor Kazu have. So I think it's wonderful."

"You think so?"

"If Kei were alive, I'm sure the place would be much merrier, don't you think?"

"That's for sure."

"It's been two years now. Time goes by so fast."

"Yeah."

Fumiko and Nagare were looking at a photo frame on the cash register. In it was a photo of Kei smiling.

Kei was Nagare's wife, who had passed away shortly after giving birth to Miki. Bright-eyed and spontaneous, her innocent, free-spirited nature allowed her to quickly befriend anyone.

As Fumiko admired the photo, she recalled what Kazu had said earlier.

Maybe I shouldn't talk to Nagare about it and worry him. It might be best to pretend for now I didn't hear it.

Fumiko nodded, as if trying to convince herself.

"Oh, right! What would you do, Nagare?"

"Sorry, what?"

"This is completely hypothetical, of course. But say you and Kei decided to split up, and when you talked it over with Miki, she cried terribly. But Miki wanted you and Kei to be happy, so she didn't admit that she didn't want you to split up and smiled instead...but then started crying. Would you and Kei still split up?"

After listening with arms crossed to Fumiko deliver the entire scenario in one quick blurb, Nagare lifted one eyebrow and muttered, "Gosh, Fumiko, I have no idea what you just said." He gazed at her, tilting his head in puzzlement.

"What? Oh, come on..."

"I'll say this, though. Even if I told Kei that I wanted to split up, she'd refuse to. Whether Miki cried or not would have nothing to do with it."

Fumiko's expression turned serious.

"What? Now you're just boasting."

"I'm not saying it to boast. I'm just telling you how it is."

"Yes, you are boasting."

"Oh, come on. You asked me."

Nagare's face had turned red with embarrassment. From the cash register, Kei was eternally beaming joyfully.

The third summer since Kei had made her trip to the future was about to start.

Some days later, Morita visited the café alone. Fumiko was not there to hear the news. So he told Kazu, who was busy behind the counter with one of her routine tasks.

"My grandson has decided to live with me. Aside from being concerned for his mom and dad, it turns out he is also worried about me, maybe because I lost my wife two years ago."

"What a kind boy."

"Yes, he really is."

After saying that, Morita left the café. He was in and out before the sweat on his forehead dried.

ii

The Nameless Child

Taira no Ason Oda Kazusanosuke Saburo Nobunaga.

That, believe it or not, is the full name of the notable historical figure Oda Nobunaga, a powerful daimyo who achieved many military victories in his quest to unify Japan. It includes his clan's name, family's name, personal name, official title, and adult name.

Names were particularly complicated in Oda Nobunaga's day. There were childhood names that individuals went by before receiving their adult name, and many warlords had different names throughout their lives. For example, the daimyo who carried on Oda Nobunaga's vision of a united Japan was Toyotomi Hideyoshi. He was also known by the completely different name of Kinoshita Tokichiro during one period in his life, and his full name was Toyotomi no Ason Hashiba Hideyoshi.

In Japan, today, just the surname and given name have

survived the flow of time. The surname represents the family's name, while the given name evolved from the person's adult name, which was also known as the secret name because people used to avoid calling each other by their adult names, as they were typically only used by those who could wield power over the other person. In Oda Nobunaga's time, only parents or lords could call someone by their adult name. Now, when he is portrayed in TV dramas or novels, he is referred to as Lord Nobunaga. It is a nice easy name for viewers or readers, but it's implausible he was referred to like that in life.

When a baby is born in Japan today, the birth must be registered within fourteen days. Once registered, the name can only be changed for a valid reason. Typically, the name is used from birth until death.

Parents would be advised to give some thought to this important task beforehand, but if they did not, some may find just fourteen days to be not nearly enough time. Especially if the husband you were meant to be choosing a name together with had died in an accident.

"So, if I go back, I can take my baby back with me… Interesting," Megumi Sakura said softly as she gazed down at her baby asleep in the pram.

Present in the café, besides Megumi, were Nagare Tokita, behind the counter wearing his white cook's uniform, and Fumiko Kiyokawa, sitting at the middle table.

Nana Kohtake, standing next to Megumi, added, "She insists that her late husband name the child, so I thought I might accompany her to keep an eye on things."

Kohtake, a café regular, worked as a nurse at a hospital nearby. She also had experienced traveling back in time. It was a journey she made one summer three years earlier, to meet her husband before he lost his memory to Alzheimer's disease.

Megumi lived in an apartment near the café. Her baby daughter was born at the hospital where Kohtake worked. Her husband, Riuji Sakura, was a victim of a fatal assault just before the birth of their child.

"She has to register the birth tomorrow, so today is her last chance," Kohtake added to emphasize the urgency of Megumi's situation.

After giving birth, a mother's body is said to have sustained damage comparable to a car crash. Her uterus suffers the most. As the placenta peels off, it leaves a circular wound of about thirty centimeters in diameter. Mothers take about six to eight weeks to regain a pre-pregnancy state of health. Everyone's experience is unique, but some need pain medication for the first two or three weeks just to be able to move about.

For Megumi, the delivery went relatively smoothly, if an eight-hour labor could be called that. Then, right after giving birth, she declared, "I want to go back in time." But such words were not something her parents could take seriously.

Megumi had an ally in Kohtake, however, who had actually returned to the past. After listening to what Kohtake had to say, Megumi's parents ultimately consented, mainly because Megumi so strongly insisted. They agreed on one condition: that Kohtake accompany her to the café.

Megumi was still experiencing pain and was unable to sit comfortably without medication, but her determination to go back in time to have her husband name their child outweighed her discomfort. As an avid fan of urban legends, Megumi and her husband had visited the café on several occasions, and she was fairly well-versed in the rules of time travel. Coming to the café today, though, the first thing she wanted to confirm was whether she could take her baby back with her. There was only one chair for which time travel was possible. No other chair allowed it, not even the one opposite. Logically, then, the trip to the past was something just one person could do. However, she wanted so dearly to show her baby to Riuji, even if just for a moment.

"I believe you might be able to" was Nagare's simple

reply to her question. "Though I'm not certain, as no one has ever done it before," he added quickly while rubbing his temple.

"Okay. I understand." Megumi nodded calmly, as if she had anticipated Nagare's answer.

This was a loophole. Any case not covered explicitly by the rules was a potential loophole. In this case, there was no rule stating that only one person could go back in time. So, presented with a scenario that the rules did not explicitly cover, Nagare could only answer that it might be possible.

Perhaps, if it wasn't a baby but two adults, each half on the seat, they might both be able to go back in time. To something like that, which no one had ever tried, Nagare could only reply vaguely.

Fumiko was listening in on the conversation, and spoke up.

"But have you thought this through? Putting myself in your husband's shoes, I think I would suspect something bad will have happened to me."

Megumi didn't answer. She looked down at her sleeping child in the pram.

Fumiko continued: "For example, why not go back alone and ask your husband what name he plans to give to your child? That way, you might accomplish what you set out to do without letting on that he died, don't you think?"

What Fumiko was trying to say was that if Megumi appeared with their baby and asked Riuji to name her, his immediate thought would be: "Why am I not there to name her? Does that mean I die?" As he shared his wife's love of urban legends, his intimate knowledge of the café and its time-bending abilities only increased the odds of such an outcome.

In other words, if Megumi went back in time with the baby, it would be like announcing Riuji's death.

Megumi exchanged glances with Kohtake.

"You're right. Maybe I'm just thinking about myself. But still..."

"But still?"

"I want him to have seen our child. Even if only once, for a momentary embrace. How could my husband not have wanted that? I'm certain it would have been his wish." Saying this, Megumi gently stroked her sleeping baby's head. Reacting to her touch, the baby twitched but kept her eyes closed.

Fumiko felt ashamed of her shallow question. "I'm sorry," she mumbled, shrinking in her seat.

As Fumiko hung her head in dejection, Kohtake approached her.

"You know, I told her just the same. And I got the

same reply, which made me stop and think, same as you. Our reasoning seems to miss the point. Putting myself in her shoes, I might do the same. After all, the baby is irresistibly cute. If I knew I could show the baby to him, I'd want to seize that opportunity."

"I agree. I'd want to do so, too." Fumiko nodded wholeheartedly to Kohtake's words of support and peered at the baby lying in the pram. "So cute."

Just then, the baby began to fuss and Fumiko jumped back, thinking she had made her cry. "Ah, I'm sorry!"

Megumi, who was new to mothering, looked to Kohtake for help, unsure what to do.

"Don't worry. Everything's okay," said Kohtake to reassure Megumi as she expertly picked up the baby in Megumi's place. "There, there," she said while gently patting the baby's bottom.

"She doesn't need changing."

"Sorry, Kohtake, I should be doing this."

Though she spoke apologetically, her expression clearly showed relief that Kohtake had accompanied her. The baby's face reddened quickly as she cried out in strained bursts.

"Perhaps the little one is a bit hungry?" Kohtake said, turning to Nagare.

"Shall I prepare some milk? Do you have some formula and a bottle?"

"Eh? But..."

Confused by Nagare's words, Megumi looked to Kohtake for guidance.

"Oh, don't worry. You wouldn't be imposing," Kohtake replied reassuringly. "Thanks, Nagare, that would be great," she said in place of Megumi. She untied a drawstring cloth bag from the pram and handed it to Nagare. It contained some formula and a bottle that Megumi had prepared at her suggestion.

"Sorry to be a bother," said Megumi with an appreciative nod.

"Please wait a moment. I'll prepare it right away," Nagare said before disappearing into the kitchen.

"I'm really sorry about this," muttered Megumi, and she stared at the entrance to the kitchen long after Nagare was out of sight.

As regular customers, Fumiko and Kohtake knew that Nagare was simply acting out of kindness. However, it was understandable that Megumi might feel uneasy about whether it was appropriate to ask the staff of a café to mix up some formula for her baby.

Fumiko tried to reassure her. "You don't have to worry about that. Preparing baby bottles is very much part of Nagare's repertoire."

"Is that so?" Megumi replied, but thought to herself with a bitter smile, *That's not what I'm concerned about.*

"What are we going to name the baby?" Riuji Sakura asked Megumi, who was sitting in the front passenger seat. They had stopped at an intersection in the northwestern area of inner Tokyo. An overpass carrying a major arterial road loomed above them.

"We have only just found out I'm pregnant. It's a little early for names, don't you think?" Megumi replied, rubbing her not-yet-swollen belly.

"If it's a boy, what about a key figure in Japanese history, like Nobunaga?"

"Oh, please tell me you're kidding?"

"Why? I think that would be a cool name."

"Absolutely not. It might be okay if we were living in those sword-fighting feudal days. But not now. Let's choose a more regular name."

"All right. Then what do you suggest?"

"Let's wait at least until we know if it's a boy or a girl."

"Why not think of names for both?"

"That doesn't appeal to me."

"Why not?"

"I just think that if, say, it turns out to be a boy, the name we chose for a girl wouldn't be used. So even though we chose that name for our unborn child, it would be as if it never existed. It just feels sad for that name."

The red light changed to green, and the surrounding cars began moving slowly. After a slight delay, Riuji also hit the accelerator.

"Yeah, I guess you're right. It's just like you to make a good point, Megumi. Let's decide on a name after the baby is born!" His voice had turned a tone brighter.

"No, we don't have to wait that long. I'm just saying let's think about it after we know the sex of the baby in a few months."

Megumi was used to Riuji's extreme changes of opinion. His impulsivity at such times was more like that of a child than a reasoning adult, but it was that innocent charm that drew Megumi to him. Although he was two years older, she found him cute. If Riuji thought Megumi was right, he would quickly backpedal on what he'd said. Willing to accept the reality of the situation, he didn't let his pride prevent him from enjoying good times or pursuing things he believed were good. He readily offered a genuine apology if he thought he was wrong. But when he believed he was right, he wouldn't back down. He was like a kid in an adult's body.

Megumi called Riuji a "kidult," a term she coined. She thought it suited him well.

"No, what I'm trying to tell you is that we should opt

to not know until it is born. Not knowing whether it is a boy or girl until then would be like a surprise that our baby brings into the world. Just thinking about it has made me excited with anticipation!"

"Oh, come on! What would your parents have to say about that? Everyone finds out their child's gender before it's born nowadays. It's essential for planning gifts for the baby shower."

"I can't see the problem. I'll just say, 'I can't tell you!'"

"That might work with your parents..." *Actually, I think it would work. They raised him, and they sometimes seem even more kidult than him.* "...but it won't work with mine!"

"Why not? Don't they like surprises?"

"That's not the reason..." said Megumi. She paused for a moment. Her expression darkened, and her voice became quieter. "Well, to be honest, that is actually why. My parents hate surprises. I don't mean dislike; it's a trauma for them."

"Trauma?"

"When I was young, my parents planned a surprise for my sister. They pretended to have forgotten to buy her a birthday cake. But before they could let her know it was a surprise joke, my sister ran out of the house. She was missing for three days. Ever since then, any kind of surprise is taboo at our house."

Megumi's story was mostly true. What actually happened was that her sister only pretended to run away and soon returned, intending to give her parents a bigger surprise than they had given her. Megumi had told Riuji a slightly embellished version of this story to change his mind. The tactic might not have worked. But Riuji was a kidult.

"All right then, surprises are a no-go."

Taking Megumi's story to heart, Riuji slumped despondently as he gripped the steering wheel with both hands. Megumi also looked downcast, but she was thinking, *The kidult is so easily persuaded.*

This rather heavy atmosphere lingered as the car entered a more bustling commercial area. They waited at a red light in the left-turn lane at the main intersection of Jimbocho.

"Okay, I've got it. Just don't tell me! Tell everyone not to tell me, and it will be just my surprise. How about that?"

Riuji hadn't given up on the surprise. While the car was still stationary, he took the opportunity to lean in close to Megumi and beamed at her with sparkling eyes.

Was he quiet just now because he was waiting for the right moment to say this?

Megumi thought about it. She was dealing with the

kidult, so she could expect him to sulk if she didn't accept his proposal.

He's bound to change his mind eventually.

She pretended to think seriously for a moment before saying, "Sure, why not. I can just tell Mom and Dad to keep it a secret from you. Let's go with that plan!"

"Great!"

Riuji bobbed up and down excitedly in the driver's seat. They were still waiting for the light to turn green, but Megumi was genuinely worried that he would accidentally step on the accelerator.

"Then let's wait until our child is born before we think of a name."

"What?"

"Let's decide on a name together then. After all, I won't know whether it is a boy or girl until that time."

"Why don't we think of a name for either case?" *Although I will know the baby's gender beforehand.*

"Wait. Didn't you just say you were against that idea?"

At some point in the conversation, Megumi's and Riuji's positions had flipped. The conversation had somehow just flowed that way, but... *I messed up*, Megumi thought as she winced awkwardly in frustration.

"All right, we'll decide on the name together after the baby is born."

"Great!"

Megumi let out a small sigh. She was sensing that her parents were already waiting eagerly for the Seventh Night, the traditional time to announce a baby's name, and other such rituals. They were waiting for their first adorable grandchild and had already shared a few potential names with her.

But when I think about it, it's a name that our child will carry for their entire life.

Megumi wanted to decide with Riuji. She had never even imagined that Riuji would not be there to do so, not until that fateful day…

The café's middle pendulum wall clock chimed *dong, dong, dong* to announce that it was three in the afternoon. Nagare returned from the kitchen lightly shaking the baby's bottle.

At the very same moment, Miki, who had been napping in the back room, appeared. Nagare's daughter Miki, who turned two this spring, seemed to be still sleepy by the way she was rubbing her eyes.

"Oh, you're up?"

"Three o'clock is snack time."

Nagare glanced ruefully at the clock.

"You know the schedule too well. Wait a moment. I'll just do this first," he said with a sigh.

"Okay, monsieur."

"Where did you learn that?"

Ignoring Nagare's grumbling, Miki climbed onto the chair opposite the woman in the white dress and waited for her snack.

Seated at the table behind Miki was Fumiko, with whom Miki had a close connection. The two began engaging in odd conversation.

"Fumiko."

"What?"

"Did you lose your job?"

"I did not."

"You are here every day."

"I'm in love with this café."

"Are you going to marry the café?"

"Not that kind of in love."

"What kind of in love?"

"As in it's my favorite spot."

"Favorite pot?"

"S. P. O. T., spot."

"Spot spot spot s pots pots pots…pots pans cans fans vans!"

"Are we playing a word game?"

"Vans!"

"Vans? Vans…vans…vans…"

Fumiko fell deep into thought.

Frowning confusedly from Miki and Fumiko's conversation, Nagare handed the bottle to Kohtake, who was holding the baby.

"Sorry to be such a bother," said Megumi at Kohtake's side. She bowed her head apologetically.

"I've prepared it slightly less warm than usual."

"Thank you so much."

The temperature of the milk given to newborns is said to be just right at around human body temperature. Nagare, a chef, prepared the milk at a slightly lower temperature of 33–34 degrees Celsius, using a thermometer. He believed this was the most reassuring temperature for a baby. Though it was just his own theory, this conviction was born out of his experience preparing milk for Miki.

"What about my snack?"

"Miki, let's play that word game."

"What word game?" Miki asked, looking confused.

Fumiko drooped despondently. Their conversations always proceeded at Miki's pace. Kohtake chuckled as she observed the interaction between the two.

Nagare showed no interest in their conversation, but rather sighed and said, "I'll get you a snack," as he went back to the kitchen.

"What are you reading today?"

In a burst of spontaneity, Miki stood up on the chair, reached over, and grabbed the book that the woman in the white dress was reading. She wanted to flip it over to reveal the cover.

"No, Miki, stop!" said Fumiko hastily. Stopped in her tracks, the now wide-eyed Miki looked back questioningly at Fumiko.

"You mustn't touch the lady's book."

Miki blinked her large eyes repeatedly. She had no idea why Fumiko was so flustered.

Fumiko continued, "You know it's dangerous to do that, right?" She had stopped Miki not because she thought standing on the chair was dangerous, or bad manners. It was because she knew that the woman in the white dress was a ghost, and she was well aware of what she was capable of doing.

Three years earlier, Fumiko had experienced first-hand how it felt to be cursed when she had forcibly tried to pull the woman from her chair to go back to the past. She remembered the moment when the woman glared at her with a bloodcurdling look. It was like she was being crushed by an enormous invisible mass of air, pushing her to the floor and making her feel suffocated and unable to speak. On that occasion, she was rescued by Kazu Tokita.

I can't let Miki have such a terrifying experience. With that thought, Fumiko had spoken out to protect Miki from the curse.

"Miki dear, let go of the lady's book."

Still holding on to the book, Miki peered back expressionlessly at Fumiko. Then ignoring Fumiko's efforts to stop her, she took the book from the woman in the white dress.

She'll be cursed! Fumiko screamed in her heart as she closed her eyes.

"?"

But nothing happened. No café lights were suddenly flickering like candles, and no eerie voices of groaning spirits were echoing through the air, as had happened when Fumiko was cursed. The ceiling fan spun quietly. And if one took the time to listen, the ticking of the clocks was the dominant sound.

Why?

What surprised Fumiko the most was how the woman in the white dress, who had just been rudely separated from her book, was sipping her coffee calmly as if nothing had happened.

With a puzzled expression, Miki was staring at the book cover. Still only two, she couldn't read yet.

"What are you doing?" asked Nagare as he returned from the kitchen. He was holding a custard pudding that had been set in a jar. Fumiko continued to stare at Miki, whose eyes had lit up upon seeing it.

Without as much as a sideways glance to Fumiko, Nagare said, "Give Kaname back her book. And no more standing on chairs."

He placed the pudding in front of Miki.

"Yes, monsieur."

After returning the book, Miki sat on her chair and snatched the custard pudding. The jar, which had appeared to be the size of a bottle cap in Nagare's hand, now looked like a rice bowl in Miki's.

"Um…"

"What is it, Fumiko?"

"Why wasn't Miki cursed this time?" Fumiko's gaze was intense as she pressed Nagare for an answer. "Is it due to her being of Tokita lineage?"

"It's unrelated to that."

"Then why?"

"Only those who want to go back to the past get cursed."

"What?"

"When you were cursed, it was when you were wishing to return to the past, right?"

"Yes."

"That was why you were cursed. But Miki doesn't have a desire to go back."

"And that's why she wasn't cursed."

"Correct."

As Fumiko was looking at Miki enjoying her pudding, her expression suddenly changed as if the meaning had sunk in.

"Then if I were to take the book away now?"

"You won't be cursed."

Wasting no time, Fumiko grabbed the book from the hands of the woman in the white dress. And, indeed, nothing happened.

"It's true!"

Fumiko jumped about joyfully, while the woman in the white dress gazed into space with an empty expression.

"Yes, but in your case, Fumiko, you've already returned to the past, so it doesn't matter."

"What?"

"Well, there is no second time, so you can't be cursed."

"What do you mean?"

"Oh, did no one ever tell you? You can only return to the past once."

"I never knew that."

"Yeah, one time only."

"Just once?"

"Only once."

"For real?"

"Yes, for real."

"But how come I've never heard this before?"

"Well, we don't consider it one of the rules because it's just a matter of fact."

"How is it not a rule?"

"Well, a rule is something you need to obey. If you try to break a rule, you can. But this is just a matter of fact. It is how it is."

"So?"

"You can't go back to the past again, Fumiko."

"What about the future?"

"Absolutely not."

"Oh, no."

Fumiko staggered backward and sat back down in her chair, lowering her head dejectedly.

The bottle was almost empty. Megumi's mind was far away as she stared at her baby in Kohtake's arms. She was yet to notice the milk was down to its final drops.

Maybe that woman and Kohtake are right. Am I seriously going to bring the baby to meet him? I can just go back alone and ask him. No one would want to learn they were about to die. Riuji certainly wouldn't…but.

People are constantly wavering as they live their lives. There is never a decision made that leaves a person entirely free from doubt. That doubt is like a second person residing in one's heart. Cartoons often depict such a thing as an angel and devil, but both are speaking from the heart.

Within Megumi's heart, two facets of herself were battling it out.

This is Riuji; he would be fine. Why, he would even thank me for bringing the baby along.

That's just how you choose to imagine it. If you bring the baby, it will be a clear message that he has died. How do you expect to conceal that from him?

I won't conceal it. I will speak honestly.

That's why I say it's selfish of you! There's a good chance he would be happier not knowing the truth. But you insist on disregarding this and revealing everything. Why is it that you constantly consider Riuji's feelings now that he's dead, while neglecting to consider his emotions when he was still alive?

This internal exchange had taken place repeatedly since the birth.

Why do I feel such doubt now, of all times? Megumi thought as she closed her eyes.

People's hearts are forever changing. However firm one's resolve might be, even the most trivial event can trigger doubt. And once a doubt has seen the light of day, it can be difficult to suppress, however hard one tries. It is as if a different version of oneself has suddenly emerged with opposite views from seconds earlier. Why had she begun to waver just now? Even Megumi herself could not explain it.

"Is everything okay?"

Sensing Megumi's mood, Nagare spoke up. It was then that Megumi finally noticed the empty bottle.

"Oh, finished already… Sorry, and thank you," she said, lowering her head to Nagare. With her eyes now closed, the baby seemed content in Kohtake's arms.

"If my wife were alive and here…" Nagare said with his gaze directed at the photo frame on the counter. The photo was of his wife, Kei Tokita.

"Pardon?"

Megumi couldn't hide her confusion that Nagare was suddenly talking about his wife. Despite noticing her bewilderment, Nagare continued, "I think she would say that you should go back to see him."

"Yes, Kei would definitely say that," chimed in Kohtake from alongside Megumi, whose eyes were open wide in surprise at Nagare's remarks.

"Why do you say that?" asked Megumi.

Nagare scratched his head. His eyes narrowed even further.

"I'm no good at engaging in the personal affairs of others and tend to avoid commenting on their actions, but my wife was the complete opposite. If she were here now, I think she would say, 'You should go.'"

"Why?" Megumi inquired. Her gaze was fixed on the photo in the frame. Kei's lively eyes sparkled, and warmth radiated from her smile.

"My wife went to see someone, too. It was to the future, in her case."

"Really?"

"My wife was frail and had been told she could not expect to live long if she gave birth to her child. Her reason for visiting the future was to make sure her child was living happily." Nagare was looking at Miki as he said "her child."

"I was against it," Nagare continued. "It was possible that she would visit a future where her child was never born. But my wife did visit the future. And she returned smiling."

"At that time..." began Kohtake in a low voice. "If she had not gone to the future to meet Miki, then even after safely delivering her, she would have constantly cried, forever anxious about the future."

"Yes, that's true," Nagare agreed with a wry smile as he remembered his attempt to dissuade Kei from going to the future. He was now glad she did make that decision. "That's why I think if my wife were here, seeing you still unsure, she would say you should go."

"That's exactly what she told me," Kohtake concurred with a shrug.

"Oh, really?" Nagare mused.

Kohtake had experienced going back to the past, too. She had gone back to receive a letter that her husband had held on to dearly. Alzheimer's had eroded his memory and identity, so he had missed the chance to deliver it to her.

At that time, Kohtake had wavered. She was unsure whether her present self should receive a letter written to her past self. But Kei had encouraged her and told her to go and receive it.

"Don't worry. Believe in yourself. Believe in your husband. In life, there are only two paths: to act or not to act. Humans must choose one. I went. Kei did, too," said Kohtake.

"As did I," added Fumiko, looking at Megumi determinedly.

"If you don't go, I think you'll regret it whenever you call your child's name. So, I believe you should go. Go and have your husband name your child. Do it so you can live with pride, knowing that your husband chose the name." Kohtake smiled gently at Megumi.

"Understood." Megumi nodded with conviction.

They're right. If I don't go, I'm sure to regret it. So, if I go, I should speak freely. There's no point in trying to conceal the truth.

Megumi's gaze locked on to the seat where the woman in the white dress was sitting.

"I've decided to go. I'm finished with the doubting."

"That's the spirit," Kohtake said supportively with another smile, while Nagare and Fumiko exchanged glances.

Just then, Miki finished her pudding and clasped her hands together, saying, "Thank you for the meal."

Two hours had crawled by. To return to the past, Megumi had to wait for the woman in the white dress to visit the toilet, but she didn't know when that would happen. Opening hours for the café Funiculi Funicula were ten in the morning to eight in the evening, but there was no guarantee that the woman would visit the toilet then. It could be midnight or early morning. Even a statistician would struggle to make sense of such irregular and unpredictable timing. If she wanted to go back to the past, she simply had to wait.

Dong, Dong, Dong, Dong, Dong.

One of the clocks chimed five times.

For two hours, no new customers had entered the café. Megumi was now the only one. Fumiko had returned to work, and Kohtake had suddenly dashed off, saying she would be back shortly: the local police had called her to let her know her husband with Alzheimer's was under their care. Now there was only Kazu Tokita. Kazu had returned to take over from Nagare, who was out shopping with Miki.

Kazu was standing quietly behind the counter, making no particular effort to engage in conversation. Megumi was sitting at the table closest to the entrance, gently rocking the pram back and forth as she waited for the seat to become vacant.

Kohtake had worried about Megumi's post-partum condition, but Megumi had not exhibited signs of fatigue. And although her newborn daughter had been fussing every now and then, she now slept peacefully.

I so badly want Riuji to see her. He can choose her name.

The doubt in Megumi's heart had vanished.

Then it happened.

Flap.

The soft sound of a book being closed could be heard from the back of the café. Megumi looked over to the source of the sound to see the woman in the white dress slowly standing up.

"Ah..."

That utterance, which escaped Megumi's lips involuntarily, was, after two hours of waiting, her inner voice saying, *Finally, she's moving.* She found herself glancing around the café, searching for Kohtake despite knowing she wasn't there.

The woman has finally got up from her seat, but…

The person Megumi dearly wanted there by her side just then was Kohtake, who together with Nagare had encouraged her by saying, "You should go." But she knew the woman in the white dress would not wait for that. She watched the woman, with book in hand, pass by her side silently and disappear toward the toilet.

Megumi turned to Kazu behind the counter for guidance.

"Go ahead."

Without any change in expression, Kazu quietly urged Megumi toward the empty seat.

"Right, then."

Megumi gently lifted her daughter from the pram, being careful not to wake her, and tentatively approached the seat until she was standing before it.

If I sit here, I can see Riuji.

With her daughter in her arms, Megumi sat down, sliding in between the table and the chair.

As soon as she did so, she noticed a coolness to the air enveloping her. She took a look around the café, and the first thing she laid eyes on was a pendulum wall clock. It was the middle one of the café's three clocks.

Megumi checked her watch. Only the clock in the

middle was keeping correct time. The other two were showing different times, and their hands were frozen in place.

They seem to be broken, she thought, tilting her head in curiosity.

"I assume you are familiar with the rules?"

Megumi suddenly became aware of Kazu standing next to her. On the tray in her hands were a gleaming silver kettle and a coffee cup.

"Um, y-yes."

Kazu lifted the pure white coffee cup from the tray and gently placed it in front of Megumi.

"I will now pour your coffee. You can only remain in the past from the moment the cup is filled with coffee until the moment the coffee gets cold. Is that understood?"

Kazu explained this matter-of-factly with a clear, calm voice devoid of intonation.

"Yes, I understand."

Though I never believed it was actually possible to go back in time.

Megumi shrugged her shoulders subtly, so as not to draw attention from Kazu, as she gazed at the empty cup.

"I'm sure you heard from my cousin, but when you go back in time, be sure you are not separated from your child. If you do, only your child will return from the past to the present."

Megumi had heard this earlier from Nagare: "Just make sure you are holding some part of your baby all the time."

"I understand," Megumi replied, pressing her cheek against her daughter's head as she cradled her against her chest.

"Then I shall begin pouring," Kazu said, holding the silver kettle in front of her. "Remember, before the coffee gets cold," she whispered.

At that moment, Megumi felt a rising tension in the atmosphere. Clearly, it wasn't just due to her own nervousness; she perceived a distinct change around her.

In front of her eyes, a stream of coffee poured from the silver kettle into the cup. Then steam rose from the filled cup, forming a wispy trail. As her eyes followed the trail floating upward, she was suddenly overwhelmed by a powerful dizziness that made it feel like the world was spinning. The scene around her distorted and began cascading downward. For a moment, she couldn't grasp what was happening and panic set in.

Megumi looked down to see her hands, and her daughter she was holding, had transformed into wisps of steam, hovering in midair. Fearing her daughter might slip away, she tightly embraced her now vaporous baby with her own vaporous hands and arms.

In the next moment, Megumi's body was sucked up into the ceiling at a speed reminiscent of a thrilling roller-coaster ride.

"I want you to change jobs."

The fact that Megumi's husband, Riuji, was a fire-fighter caused her constant worry. In addition to the regular task of putting out fires, a firefighter's role also involved rescue work during natural emergencies such as earthquakes and typhoons. After she was pregnant, each time Megumi saw a news report of a disaster on TV she raised the subject of changing careers.

"I'll be fine. You worry too much, Megumi."

"But…"

"Of course people have lost their life in the line of duty, but last year, out of a hundred and sixty thousand staff members, only seven died."

"I know, but…"

"So don't worry. I'll be fine. To protect people, to save lives, that's a firefighter's duty. You know… I told you before how that sense of duty has always appealed to me, right? It just struck a chord with me when I read it as a kid…"

"Yes. Yes. I understand!" Megumi said in surrender and looked up in exasperation. She didn't actually think Riuji would die in the line of duty. It was simply worrying for her. Riuji was clearly aware of that, too.

"You can set your mind at ease. I'm not going to die, okay? There's no way I would leave this child behind and die, right?" Riuji said as he gently stroked Megumi's still-not-so-big stomach.

Megumi sighed deeply.

Riuji's aspiration to become a firefighter was sparked by a comic he read as a child. The protagonist of this particular story wasn't a firefighter, but Riuji was influenced by a line in one panel spoken by a firefighter who had rescued a child from a fire scene. He was asked by the protagonist, "Why did you choose such a dangerous job?" The firefighter replied, "To protect people, to save lives, that's a firefighter's duty. Today it was my duty to save this child's life."

Upon reading this line, a jolt of inspiration surged through Riuji's mind.

So cool! I want to protect people and save lives like a firefighter.

Megumi had heard this story dozens or even hundreds of times. Partly this was because she had often told him that he should consider changing his line of work. She did so not in the belief that he would, but rather as a way to express her worry.

Ironically, a cruel twist of fate was in store for Riuji.

Megumi had returned to her parents' home in Fukushima before she gave birth. Her parents still used a black telephone, a dial-type model that rang loudly when there was an incoming call. Megumi's childhood home was a traditional farmhouse. Until it had been rebuilt a few years ago, it still had a thatched roof. The unique features of a traditional farmhouse are its square single-story layout comprised of four evenly sized square rooms, providing a spacious feel; its scarcity of windows, leaving the interior dimly lit; and its use of crooked timber for pillars and other structural elements.

The house had a living room, a guest room, a bedroom, and a workroom, and nearly all the walls were earthen.

However, the house was damaged by the 2011 Great East Japan Earthquake, with some parts of it collapsing, and it had to be rebuilt. As the original wooden pillars and beams were intact, they were reused to transform the house into a semi-traditional-style home. When Megumi visited her parents, she could still feel the remnants of the old house scattered throughout. Although it had been renovated, it was still a place where she truly could feel she was back home.

One of the reasons she decided to stay with her parents before the birth of their child was that she was becoming increasingly irritated at Riuji's childish behavior.

He hadn't been opposed to her going. But being in a contrarian mood, he exclaimed, "Yes! I get to live solo for the first time in ages," which rubbed Megumi the wrong way.

He meant nothing by it. It was simply what entered his head. He lacked tact, but that was all he could be criticized for. If it wasn't for the fact that Megumi would soon be giving birth for the first time, she probably would have laughed and let it slide. But she couldn't. It was exactly why she needed some space. She left the city to distance herself from Riuji, and she found solace in peaceful days surrounded by her parents and grandparents.

One day, the black telephone rang loudly and Megumi's grandmother answered it. Seeing her hard-of-hearing grandmother asking the caller to repeat themselves over and over, Megumi stepped in and took the receiver. Her grandmother stood by worriedly, sensing an unsettling vibe from the scattering of words she did hear.

"Yes, that's my husband... What?"

All color drained from Megumi's face.

The police informed her that Riuji had intervened in a fight on the train during his commute home, and a passenger in a wild rage had slashed his neck with a box-cutter knife. He bled profusely and passed away.

Megumi had no memory of what happened between putting the receiver down and seeing Riuji's face as he lay in the mortuary. She didn't know how she left the house, how she traveled, or how she arrived at the police station. She didn't even recall that her father and mother accompanied her.

According to her mother, Megumi never lost her composure or became distraught, calmly responding to their questions. It wasn't until they reached the police station and saw Megumi enter the mortuary that her parents realized there had been no mistake about the tragic news.

Immediately after that, Megumi went into labor. And when she came face-to-face with her newborn daughter in the delivery room, she burst into a flood of tears.

When Megumi opened her eyes, she saw Riuji sitting at the table opposite hers, looking at her with sparkling eyes. "Oh. Hey, you!"

"What…? What?"

She had expected that Riuji would be startled by her sudden appearance, but she was the one caught by surprise. She had not been expecting him to believe that she had come from the future just like that.

Riuji came over to her table.

"Megumi, you were sitting in front of me just a moment ago. Then I blinked...and now you're sitting here. How did you do that?"

Well, it's no wonder you're puzzled. But you're looking at me as if I'm a ghost or something. Yet I'm probably more startled to be seeing you.

It was indeed a shock. Megumi had seen Riuji lying in the mortuary. She remembered placing flowers on the body in the coffin. They were cold hard facts that could not be reversed.

Yet Riuji was here in front of her. She almost screamed in disbelief.

"...I guess that means you've come from the future?"

"That's right."

As lovers of urban legends, the two of them were originally attracted to this café by the rumor of its ability to allow customers to go back in time, and they had visited occasionally, so of course they were well aware of the rules. Now that Megumi was sitting in the seat that could take you back to the past, it was only natural for Riuji to consider the possibility that the Megumi in front of him had come from the future. However, this was a big fact to swallow, and Riuji was still trying to get a handle on it.

He seemed to be in a daze as he tentatively sat down opposite Megumi.

"Um, I don't have time to explain, but listen..."

Megumi hesitated. She was torn over what to do. Should she delay the conversation about their daughter until she addressed Riuji's death, or discuss their daughter first and then break the news?

Rather than waiting for her to continue, Riuji was fixated on the coffee cup in front of him.

"Hey! Is this the coffee you have to drink before it gets cold?"

"Yes. It is."

Riuji extended his hands and placed his palm on the side of the cup to check the temperature.

"Doesn't feel very hot. Feel it. It's only lukewarm. It will be cool in no time!"

Surprised, Megumi took a sip. "You're right. It's cooling down so fast."

Her eyes widened. If Riuji hadn't mentioned it, she would have assumed it was still hot, maybe not scalding hot, but at least hot. The time she would have with him would be less than she expected.

Seven to eight minutes. A bit longer, perhaps. But the time will race by.

Human perception is subjective. Unpleasant moments feel long, while enjoyable ones feel short. Megumi looked at the clock in front of her. It showed five seventeen. She reminded herself to check the temperature again once the minute hand indicated twenty-five.

After persistently looking at the cup, Riuji suddenly proposed something outrageous.

"What would happen if I drank it?"

He had a childlike way of thinking. But that was Riuji's quirkiness.

Megumi couldn't contain her unease as she watched Riuji behave so playfully, oblivious to the fate that awaited him. He then turned his attention to Kazu behind the counter.

"Is there any rule against me drinking this?" he asked.

"Please don't ask such strange questions," scolded Megumi, thinking how childish he was to ask such a thing.

However, Kazu seemed unfazed by the question, and said with calm certainty, "That would be fine."

And indeed, although the rules stipulated that the coffee must be drunk before it got cold, it did not specify by whom.

"Awesome!" Riuji's excitement surged upon receiving this clarification.

"Settle down," Megumi said in exasperation, with a

small, sad sigh. It was a familiar exchange they had repeated many times before. But once the coffee was drunk it would be the end. Turning away from him, she wiped away the tears welling in her eyes.

"What a cute baby. Whose is it?"

Riuji finally acknowledged the presence of the baby Megumi was holding.

"Obviously, it's yours!"

"What? No way! Seriously? My child? Let me have a good look."

Riuji peered at the baby.

"It's a girl?"

"Yeah."

"She's adorable. Her eyes resemble yours, Megumi."

"Really? Her nose looks like yours."

"You think?"

"Yes, they are much alike."

"I see. That makes me happy to hear."

Seeing Riuji's face beaming with happiness as he gently stroked the baby's tiny nose, Megumi felt a wave of emotions, and tears threatened to well up in her eyes once again. Why did he have to die? Megumi knew there was no use dwelling on it, but her mind was filled with these thoughts.

"And by the way…"

"What is it?"

Riuji suddenly stared at Megumi with a serious expression she had never seen before. His eyes were intense, filled with earnestness.

Her heart beat faster.

He must have worked it out. Well, it's only natural. It's strange for me to bring our daughter to meet him. I'm sorry, Riuji. I should have told you properly.

She stiffened, waiting for his next words.

"I…I think if this kid brings a boyfriend home, I might end up punching him. Can I do that?"

"What?"

Her breath was momentarily stolen by his unexpected words.

"N-no, of course you can't. And it's way too early to be thinking such things."

"I just know I'll burst into tears at her wedding. Please, no letters to the parents, or anything like that!"

"It's too early for that, I'm saying!"

"It's no good. I can't help crying just imagining it." Riuji took a couple of steps and turned his back to Megumi.

"Oh, Riuji…"

Megumi was about to tell him to stop being over-the-top, but when she saw that he was trembling and crying, she couldn't find the words.

So, he noticed, after all.

Riuji had a childlike side, but he was also a sharp

thinker. He had excelled in shogi since he was a boy, and won several amateur competitions for elementary and junior high school students. Even after becoming a firefighter, he occasionally attended shogi classes taught by professional players. If Megumi suddenly appeared to see him at this café with a young baby, he was always going to deduce what had happened to him.

"I'm sorry," said Megumi.

"Why are you apologizing?"

"I should have told you myself." *I was scared.* "Instead, you had to work it out alone." *And part of me was expecting it to be like that.* "Did you realize it from the moment I showed up with our child in my arms?"

"...Yeah."

"I see. I kind of thought you would."

"But having you appear suddenly like this... To be honest, I was confused, and, um, how should I put it? It took time for me to accept the truth. I'm sorry."

"Why are you apologizing, Riuji? It's not your fault. It's mine, isn't it?"

"There's nothing wrong with what you did. I mean..." Riuji slowly approached Megumi's seat. "Because of you, I can meet her like this..." He trailed off, as he gently touched the baby's head.

Tears spilled from Megumi's eyes.

"You know, I've been thinking."

Gently stroking the baby's head, the back of Riuji's finger slid slowly down to her cheek.

"If it was a boy, I definitely wanted him to practice judo or karate. I wanted him to become a man who could protect a girl when the time came. I wouldn't have minded if he was a bit foolish. I just wanted him to grow up as a kindhearted man who knew what truly mattered."

"Yes," said Megumi, nodding softly as she looked up at him.

"But if it was a girl, I thought I would forgive her no matter how mischievous she was. I would become an indulgent and affectionate father. If she asked for something she wanted, I'd probably buy it for her secretly. If she wanted to go somewhere, I'd take her anywhere." His eyes were now bloodshot, but his face was filled with a smile. "But I guess that would only be while she was little. Once she entered adolescence and brought a boyfriend home, I would definitely become grumpy and be disliked by this child. I would say he's no good. We would argue. She would say she hated me, over and over again. We would end up not seeing each other for days. Maybe she would ignore me? Would I be able to endure it? Given my personality, I'd say that would be impossible, right? I would probably confront her, ask why she was ignoring me, and then she'd dislike me even more. Then what would I do...?"

"Yeah."

"But, you know, at her wedding, she would read a letter to the parents. She would thank you for giving birth to her, and tell me she was happy to be the daughter to her father..."

Riuji gently stroked the baby's head again, her wispy hair fluttering softly.

"Riuji..."

"Sorry for crying. You must have been worried, too, right?"

"No, I should be the one apologizing. I knew it all along. I'm sorry. I just really wanted you to meet your daughter."

"I understand."

"I'm really sorry."

"I understand, so don't worry about it."

Using his hand that was stroking the baby's head, Riuji wiped the tears from Megumi's cheeks.

"Riuji..."

Megumi looked up to see the pendulum wall clock directly in her line of vision. The hands, which were at five seventeen, had not moved at all.

In this café, when you travel to the past, the middle clock—the one naturally drawing your gaze from the time-traveling seat—pauses, while the left clock—the one closest to the entrance—takes over. While the middle clock had shown the correct time in the present, now it was the clock on the left that needed to be watched. Megumi had been keeping track of time by a clock that had paused.

"What is it?"

Megumi hastily touched the cup. It was colder.

"The time?"

Riuji, who knew the rules well, realized from Megumi's actions that there was little time left.

"A name."

"What?"

"I want you to name our child, Riuji. I want to be able to tell her that she was named by her father. I want her to grow up knowing that. So please, give her a name."

"...Yu."

"What?"

"Yu, meaning 'gentle.'"

"Yu?"

Riuji's reply was almost immediate.

"I've been thinking about it all along. I know I said I didn't want to know whether the baby was a boy or a girl until it was born. But I couldn't wait. I've been thinking about what name would be good. So, I chose one kanji character that could be used for a boy using the pronunciation 'Yutaka,' or for a girl using the pronunciation 'Yu.'"

"Yu."

"One reason I chose the meaning 'gentle' was that I wanted her to treat me gently and forgive me even if I punched her boyfriend."

"...How stupid."

"I'll leave it in your hands."

"...Sure."

Riuji had chosen a name infused with his wishes, a kind of consolation for yearning for the unattainable, and Megumi fully understood the sentiment.

"Come here."

Megumi urged Riuji to hold Yu. "As long as I'm touching Yu's body, it'll be okay."

"Really?"

Riuji glanced at Kazu Tokita, who stood behind the counter. She remained silent, offering only a quiet nod in response.

While Megumi held Yu's hand, Riuji held their daughter in his hands.

"Yu..." Riuji called out with tears streaming down his face. "Yu, Yu?"

He said her name again and again. "Why do I have to die? Leaving behind such a cute child. God, I beg you, please don't take me away just yet. I'm not asking for too much, like letting me stay alive until her wedding. Just let me be around long enough so that I can punch her boyfriend. Even just until she enters nursery school. Or at least let me be there for her birth. Please, I'm begging you."

Riuji pressed his tear-soaked cheek against Yu's.

"Riuji..."

Riuji's feeling of not wanting to let go transmitted through Yu's body to Megumi's hand.

Miraculously, however, even in Riuji's tight embrace, Yu was not crying. On the contrary, her small hand caressed his cheek as if she were wiping away his tears.

"Oh..."

Riuji grasped her tiny hand, and his shoulders shuddered uncontrollably.

"It's no good," he whispered softly. He closed his eyes tightly and pushed Yu away from him, back into Megumi's embrace.

"Riu..." Megumi gasped.

Riuji's reddened face had contorted. Megumi had never before glimpsed such severity in his expression.

As it turned out, I did make Riuji suffer so much.

"I—I'm...sorry..."

As Megumi tried to apologize to Riuji, he took sudden decisive action. He grabbed the coffee cup, and before Megumi could react, he drank the coffee meant for her in one gulp.

CLANK!

Riuji returned the cup to the saucer with such a force, Megumi wondered if it might shatter.

The loud noise had startled Yu and caused her to fuss. But Megumi's mind was on Riuji's actions.

"Riuji?"

Breathing heavily, Riuji took a few steps back and collapsed onto the counter behind him. All strength seemed to drain from his body. His face, which moments ago was bright red, now looked a ghastly white.

"…Why?"

"It felt cruel."

Megumi's heart froze. *I should have known better than to have come.* "You mean I shouldn't have brought our child for you to see…" Her voice trembled. *He must be mad at me.*

"No. Of course not," Riuji replied.

"Then what?"

"It seemed too cruel that you had to drink the coffee under such circumstances."

"Oh, you were talking about that?"

"Yeah, what else would I mean?"

Megumi looked up to see Riuji was smiling warmly at her.

He was thinking of me…

"Riuji…"

Megumi's vision was blurring. It was not just because

of her tear-soaked eyes. Just as when she was beginning to travel back in time, the world suddenly began to warp, and she began feeling dizzy. Her body felt light, as if floating in midair.

"Riuji!"

A realization came to Megumi at that moment. It was Riuji's kindness. That was behind his accepting her thoughts and actions. He might not have been aware of it. But she was now looking behind the actions that had earned her label kidult. What she dismissed as childish were simply examples of his kindness as he intervened to avoid disagreements and fights between them.

Not long after Megumi appeared, Riuji had asked, "What would happen if I drank it?"

Such a childish idea.

Megumi had felt a mixture of exasperation, confusion, and helplessness. But perhaps Riuji had been thinking ahead when he asked if anyone could drink the coffee. Or perhaps his behavior wasn't even consciously driven, but rather intuitive.

I couldn't bring myself to drink the coffee and leave Riuji there crying alone.

If Megumi was unable to bring herself to drink the coffee and so ended up becoming a ghost, Riuji would be the one experiencing the greatest sadness. Even though she knew it, she couldn't bring herself to drink the coffee in front of her. Knowing her personality, he must have understood the situation.

In ways like that, Riuji's kindness has been constantly protecting me.

Megumi didn't know how to express these feelings. Time was running out. But she had to say something…

"Riuji!"

"Hmm?"

Blurring further, all Megumi's surroundings except Riuji began to descend. Her body completely transformed into steam. Although he could no longer see her, her voice was still in range. But Megumi was confused, unable to find the right words for her final message to Riuji.

"I love you." "I'm happy I met you." "I was happy." *Those words aren't enough! This is our last moment. We'll never see each other again!*

The body of steam that was Megumi began to slowly rise.

I never thought I'd lose you. It happened too suddenly. I still don't want to believe it. I can't believe it. You are with me now, but when I return to the present, we'll never meet again. Why is life so cruel? It's so lonely without you. I'm so lonely. Don't die. I don't want you to die. Don't leave me alone. I'm sad, so sad. It's too sad that you are not here. I worry whether I can raise our darling daughter, Yu, properly on my own. How can

I manage without you? It makes me so anxious. The more I think about it, the more anxious I become. Please, don't let me be left alone. Don't die…

Megumi couldn't find the words to express her overflowing emotions. Her consciousness was gradually slipping away. Even as she extended her vaporous hand toward Riuji, her body was being pulled upward. The impending separation drew closer; no matter how much she tried to resist, she couldn't fight against it.

As the vapor that was Megumi rose toward the ceiling, she noticed Riuji's eyes as he looked up at her were also filled with tears, and she was surprised for a moment.

That's right, my darling Riuji. You don't want to die, either. It must be nerve-racking as you contemplate our future, imagining me raising this child without you. I could yell out right now, "Don't die. Don't leave me behind." But I know it would be painful for you. It would just make you even sadder. If I can't change the reality that you're going to die no matter how hard I try, then at least…at least in this final moment of parting, I don't want to worry you any further. What can I say to ease your kind heart?

With all the cheeriness Megumi could muster, she yelled with all her might, "If Yu ever brings a lousy guy home, I'll punch him in your place!"

She saw Riuji's eyes momentarily widen in surprise. And then Megumi's consciousness faded away. All that remained was a silence that made it feel like nothing had ever happened.

Riuji laughed with tears welling in his eyes. Then, in a soft voice, he muttered, "Make sure you do that."

"What? What did you say?"

Riuji turned round in response to the voice. It was Megumi, sitting at a table, opening a compact makeup case, applying lipstick. Where Megumi from the future had been, the woman in the white dress was now sitting.

Riuji looked around the café, but the Megumi who had been holding the baby and crying in front of him just moments ago was nowhere to be found. Now there was just the Megumi who was tilting her head with an innocent expression as she smoothly applied her lipstick. Yu was nowhere to be seen.

Riuji closed his eyes slowly to preserve the memory of what had just happened. Ahh… The warmth of holding his child was still lingering, and tears welled in his eyes once again.

"Hey, what happened just now?" said Megumi with a frown as she continued to peer into her mirror.

"Hmm? Er, well…"

Riuji took a deep breath and wiped away his tears to keep them hidden from Megumi. With his gaze fixed on the woman in the white dress, he murmured, "Just once, I wanted to experience being cursed by her."

"Oh, stop it. You are always being curious and trying everything for the sake of it. That's what children do. How many times have I told you that?"

"There's nothing wrong with adults doing it, too."

"Yes. There is. Stop it." Megumi closed the makeup case with a snap and put it back in her bag. "All right, let's go home. It's already late," she said, standing up.

"Okay, sure. I just need to use the toilet before we go."

Riuji hurriedly headed toward the toilet, doing his best to hide his face from Megumi.

"Didn't you just go?"

"First time was number one. This time…"

"Too much detail! Just go!"

As Megumi smiled, she looked at the middle pendulum clock.

It said five eighteen. Unnoticed by them, the clock nearest the entrance had stopped moving, while the middle clock had resumed ticking.

When Megumi opened her eyes, the woman in the white dress was standing right in front of her.

"Oh!" Megumi exclaimed in surprise.

The woman in the white dress showed no interest in her and curtly uttered, "Move."

"Yes, sorry." Megumi got up from her seat hastily, still holding her daughter. The woman in the white dress silently slid into the empty seat.

Megumi's eyes scanned the pendulum wall clocks. The middle clock showed slightly past nine o'clock. The clock nearest the entrance showed five seventeen, the time she had seen while she was in the past. She couldn't recall if it had been this time before she went back. She felt a sense of wonder and looked at Kazu, who had emerged from the kitchen.

"Um…"

Without making eye contact with Megumi, Kazu cleared the cup Riuji had finished, asked, "So, how was it?" and served a fresh cup of coffee to the woman in the white dress. Megumi wiped away the traces of tears on her cheek and asked, "What I experienced…it wasn't a dream, was it?"

"Do you not believe it happened?"

"No, I want to believe it was true."

"Then even if what you saw was a dream, wouldn't it still be a part of your life?"

Kazu's calm and unwavering words pierced Megumi's heart.

"I think it would!" Megumi nodded in agreement and looked down at her child in her arms. "Well then, 'Yu,' from today, this will be your name."

The ticking of the clocks could be heard reverberating faintly in the café. The minute hand of the clock nearest the entrance dropped to eighteen. Time was moving not only in the present but also in the past, heading toward the future.

iii

The Father

Everyone loves omurice (omelet on rice).

By all accounts, omurice was invented in 1925 by Shigeo Kitahashi, the owner of a Western-influenced local eatery in Namba, Osaka. His inspiration was a regular customer with a sensitive stomach and a penchant for white rice and omelets. He thought, *It makes me sad to provide this boring food day after day*, and started to serve a dish he called omurice, which was ketchup-infused rice enveloped in a delicate omelet.

The recipe is straightforward. You heat butter and sauté finely chopped onions, thin slices of bacon, mixed vegetables, and rice. Then you season it with salt, pepper, and ketchup to create a distinct ketchup rice. This rice is then covered with a lightly cooked omelet. Lately, aside from the traditional ketchup-based flavoring, some people choose to add a topping, such as demi-glace or white sauce. The dish is finished off with a garnish of parsley for a dash of color.

With just a single bite, there's a medley of flavors in your mouth, the rich egg, savory sauce, and ketchup rice infused with buttery aroma. The fluffy texture is popular not only among children but also adults, and there are many omurice specialty restaurants in Tokyo.

It was early June.

A few days into the rainy season, a couple visited the café.

"I see," said Fumio Mochizuki, the husband. He was in his late fifties, and the beginnings of gray were threading through his hair. His facial reaction to hearing the café rules was unnoticeable. He simply said, "Let's go," and stood up.

CLANG-DONG

"I'm sorry," said Kayoko, the wife, with a deep bow. She looked significantly younger than Mochizuki. So much so that one might find it hard to believe she had a twenty-four-year-old daughter.

Two cups of coffee sat at the counter. Mochizuki's cup was still an untouched, full cup of coffee.

"I apologize for taking your time," said Kayoko, rising from the counter seat and bowing once again.

"No, it's fine," responded Nagare Tokita. He received the payment and bade Kayoko goodbye. Kayoko's cup, in contrast to Mochizuki's, was empty; she had consumed her coffee to the last drop.

CLANG-DONG

"If my father opposed my marriage like that, I'd choose to elope, too," muttered Fumiko Kiyokawa with a shrug. She had been privy to the entire exchange from a table seat.

"Fumiko..." Nagare chided her softly for her impolite comment.

"But seriously, that stubborn father came into this café and said nothing more than 'I see' and 'Let's go,' and he left it to his wife to explain everything. Who does he think he is? There is no way I would tolerate him doing that."

"Easy now."

"Going by his wife's explanation, it seemed like he regretted opposing his daughter's marriage, but that's history now. Even if he were to travel back, he still seems determined to oppose it."

"Eh?"

"Did you see his face? He showed no sign of regret.

It bore the expression of someone unable to come to terms with his daughter eloping. And that's why, upon learning he can't alter reality, he left so hastily, right?"

Fumiko's disdain was clearly displayed by her scowl.

"But if he was opposed to it, he must have had his reasons?"

"I bet it was something petty."

"Such as?"

"Maybe he just didn't like the look of the man she brought home, or the man didn't greet him properly."

"I see."

"Objecting to a marriage based on your personal likes or dislikes is unacceptable."

"Are you speaking from experience?"

"It was the reverse in my case."

"The reverse?"

"Far from objecting, my parents are incessantly urging me to get married. They don't care who. If I were to elope, they might put an ad in the newspaper, maybe even a full-page announcement saying, 'Congratulations!'"

"Why the newspaper?"

"Well, if I were to elope, they wouldn't be able to get in touch with me, would they?"

"Ah, that makes sense."

Three years ago, Fumiko went back in time to the

early summer. She did so to meet Goro Katada, who had promptly left for America following a breakup conversation they had at this café.

While back in the past, Goro had asked her to wait three years. As a result, Fumiko, who would be thirty-one this year, had been patiently awaiting his return. So, any opportunity to marry Goro still seemed a little further down the road.

"Can I have a refill?"

"Sure."

Taking Fumiko's empty coffee cup, Nagare disappeared into the kitchen.

Fumiko found herself alone in the café.

Well, not entirely alone. There was a woman in a white dress sitting at the far corner seat, but you couldn't exactly call her a customer, or human, either, for that matter. She was a ghost that occupied the seat that took you back in time. Day or night, she just sat there, silently reading her book, never sleeping.

To journey back in time, you must first occupy her seat. And, obviously, to do that, it was necessary to wait for her to vacate it.

However, if you were to ask, "Could I perhaps take your seat?" she would not hear. And should you try to dislodge her by force, you would be met with a curse.

But that was not to say the chance of time travel was

zero. A fleeting opportunity to sit there arose just once each day, when she got up to go to the toilet.

A ghost needing to go to the toilet? It perplexes everyone who hears it, but it is one of the annoying rules involved in time travel.

"What are you reading today?"

Fumiko tried to get a peek at the book the woman in the white dress was reading.

That's when it happened.

Suddenly the woman in the white dress appeared to be undulating and rippling. Fumiko rubbed her eyes, thinking something was wrong with her vision.

"What? What's this?"

In the blink of an eye, the woman in the white dress was enveloped by a billowing white mist. Although Fumiko was taken aback by this surreal spectacle, she had an inkling of what was unfolding. After all, three years earlier she had had a similar experience of her own body changing into steam when she journeyed back in time.

As Fumiko was gaping in mute astonishment, a woman materialized from beneath the billowing mist.

Her name was Yoko Kawashima. She was twenty-eight but bore an air of fatigue that made her look much older. Her appearance was far from neat. The sleeves of her sweater were frayed, and her unartfully pinned-up hair lacked luster.

"Nagare! Come quickly! A woman has appeared! She has come from the future!"

Fumiko called out to Nagare in the kitchen, but he did not respond. The only sound was the grinding of coffee beans. After a while he responded quite nonchalantly.

"Ah, hold on a moment. I'm in the middle of making your freshly ground coffee."

"What? But…"

Fumiko's reaction as she encountered a person from the future for the first time contrasted greatly with Nagare's routine response.

"What should I do about this?" she asked. She took a step back and looked alternately at Nagare, who was in the kitchen, and at Yoko, who had appeared so abruptly.

"Excuse me," said Yoko to Fumiko.

"Y-yes?"

"Do you work here?"

"Er, no. I don't."

While Yoko's voice carried a hint of confusion, it was clear by Fumiko's shaky voice that she was vastly more perturbed.

"Then is there anyone else here?"

"Well, the owner is currently making coffee in the kitchen, and Kazu is in the back, putting Miki to bed. Do you know Kazu?"

"Who?"

"Most probably it was Kazu who poured the coffee that brought you here," said Fumiko, pointing to the cup in front of Yoko.

"Oh..."

"Yes. That must have been Kazu. And..." Fumiko looked around: she and Yoko were the only two in the room.

"Ah, um, I'm Fumiko Kiyokawa. As I said, I don't work here. I'm a regular at this café. I'm a systems engineer. Oh, but I've also gone back to the past. So, I understand your confusion. Nice to meet you."

"Oh... Okay."

Fumiko's sudden self-introduction had clearly left Yoko at a loss.

"I'm sorry. I began prattling on..."

"No, not at all."

"You evidently didn't come to see either Nagare or Kazu. Nor me, of course. Perhaps you are expecting someone else to turn up?"

Fumiko turned to the café's entrance, but there was no striking of the bell, no signal of someone's arrival. With the realization that it was just her and Fumiko, Yoko heaved a sigh of disappointment. Her tired face seemed to age further.

Given the annoying rules she had to accept in order to travel back in time, it stood to reason that she had a substantial motive for making such a journey. Yet whoever it was Yoko wanted to meet was not here. Her disappointment was all too transparent—even to Fumiko, whom she had just met.

"May I ask who you were hoping to meet?" Although Fumiko knew her question could provide no comfort, she felt compelled to say something in response to Yoko's despondent pose.

"...Truth be told, my father," Yoko replied with a faint sigh.

"My apologies for the delay." Nagare had abruptly reappeared from the kitchen. A slender plume of steam was rising from the freshly brewed coffee he held in his hand. "So, is this an acquaintance of yours, Fumiko?" he asked.

"No. She is not!"

"You sound cross with me."

"I am not cross."

"Er, okay. But..."

Nagare cautiously examined Fumiko's countenance.

A visitor from the future arrives, and you're casually brewing coffee!

Fumiko swallowed the words that almost escaped her lips. "We have a customer!" she said, turning to Yoko, who looked increasingly glum, and she bit her lower lip in frustration.

"Ah, understood." Nagare took in Fumiko's and Yoko's expressions, and looked around and saw there was no one else in the café. "Unfortunately, this happens sometimes."

Fumiko realized that he was saying there had been customers who'd failed to meet whoever they'd wanted to meet.

"Why would that happen?" Fumiko asked Nagare, echoing Yoko's feelings.

"Well..."

"What?"

"It comes down to the emotions of the individual."

"You mean hers?"

"Yes. If in your heart you feel reluctance to meet the someone you wish to meet, you may go back to a different time in the past than you intended. Sometimes that happens."

Fumiko turned to Yoko, but when their eyes met, Yoko looked away awkwardly. Could it be that there was a grain of truth in Nagare's words that resonated with her?

"Even if you knew the exact time you wanted to return to?" Fumiko was intent on digging deeper.

"Yes, even then. I don't know why. All I can say is that it seems that one's feelings of wanting to meet someone or not wanting to meet take precedence. We've had a few such visitors before. When asked, they admitted that part of them didn't want to meet the person."

"But..."

Fumiko tried to say something more. She thought it would be such a shame if Yoko gave up. Yet she resigned to the situation. This must be another one of the rules. She felt sorry for Yoko. Nevertheless, it seemed too cruel to send her back to the future just like that.

Perhaps sensing Fumiko's feelings, Nagare said, "I'm sorry. Maybe future me didn't explain it well enough," and he bowed his head to Yoko.

"Actually, to be honest, I might not have wanted to see my father," Yoko confessed quietly as she raised her head. "I came from four years in the future. On the night of my father's funeral, my mother told me that he once visited the café..."

"The night of his funeral?"

"Yes, he had a cerebral hemorrhage. It was quite sudden..."

"But why? Why didn't you want to see your father?" Fumiko looked puzzled.

"I left home when my father objected to my marriage, and I never went back until I was told he died."

"Gosh."

Fumiko and Nagare exchanged glances.

"Back then, I never understood why he was so against

us marrying. All attempts to convince him failed. So I decided to go ahead without his consent…"

"Wait…" Fumiko exclaimed. "Your father, could he possibly be…" With startled wide-open eyes, she again exchanged glances with Nagare. She and Nagare shared the same expression. "…a man of few words, a bit old-school, the type to think women should walk two steps behind men…? His name is Mochizuki, right?"

Fumiko's question shook Yoko.

"How do you know that?"

"He was here just now! He left before you arrived, but it wasn't even ten minutes ago—it was three or four. If I chase after them, it might not be too late!"

With these words, Fumiko sprang toward the café entrance. Her hasty action, however, had unintended consequences.

"I'll come, too…"

"No!" yelled Nagare.

Driven by the idea that she should join the chase, Yoko was swept up in Fumiko's enthusiasm and rose from her seat, but in the blink of an eye, her form morphed back into a wisp of white mist and was sucked up into the ceiling. It all happened so quickly.

"Oh, no!"

As Fumiko stood frozen in a daze, Nagare winced and muttered, "Oh, we messed up."

One of the rules of this café is that when you travel to the past, you must never leave your seat. Anyone who does is immediately pulled back to the present.

As the mist vanished, the woman in the white dress materialized. She was absorbed in her book as if nothing out of the ordinary had occurred.

"Wait…was this my fault?"

"It was just one of those things. It can't be helped."

"What can we do?"

"There's nothing that can be done now."

Staggering to the nearest table and sitting down, Fumiko buried her face in her hands. Nagare continued to stare at the coffee cup.

Why was I so against the marriage? Mochizuki was thinking while on his way from Funiculi Funicula to the station. Even though it was only early June and not quite summer, the day was unusually humid, and beads of sweat formed on his brow.

"Please."

"My answer is no."

"But why?"

"It's too soon."

"What's wrong with only knowing each other for two months?"

"There's no way I can allow it."

"But why? I don't understand."

"How can you say you know a guy like that? It's just been two months!"

"What do you mean, a guy like that?"

"I mean a guy like that. He didn't even greet me properly. Out of the blue, he casually asked for my blessing. I found it beyond disrespectful."

"Well…"

"Anyway, I won't allow the marriage. Please send him home."

"Why, though? How could you? I thought you wanted me to be happy."

Three years had gone by since then. Mochizuki couldn't forget the day he disapproved of the marriage. If his daughter, Yoko, had married the man she ran off with, her last name would now be Kawashima.

Before that day, Mochizuki had never seen his daughter resist him. Watching her large tears fall, he was taken aback to see such strong emotions in his daughter, who in his eyes had always been a child. During her elementary school years, her teachers would constantly remark, "She lacks self-direction and tends to go with the flow."

When she got to high school, she joined the judo club,

saying she couldn't turn down her friend's invitation. For a girl who was in the wind instrument club during middle school, starting judo all of a sudden was a recipe for disaster. She left in less than a month.

As she moved on to junior college, this time it wasn't a sports team she joined, but the astronomy club, again because a friend invited her. Unlike the judo club, there wasn't a clear obstacle preventing her from continuing, like it being too physically challenging, so she stayed with the astronomy club for two years.

After Yoko graduated, Mochizuki's wife, Kayoko, suggested she might have continued with band club if she chose for herself.

This same daughter, Yoko, just two months into her first job, introduced her parents to her fiancé, a complete stranger. She had apparently met him through a client at work. Even though she was his own daughter, Mochizuki couldn't help but be frustrated by how she just didn't learn. How could she repeat the same mistakes and keep saying yes to everything? She mustn't do it this time, as she would undoubtedly regret it. Of that he felt certain.

But now he regretted opposing Yoko's wishes. His actions had chased her away. He could not get in touch with her. If she was in trouble, how could he help her, or even know she needed help?

Was it me who was wrong?

With each passing day, that thought strengthened. Mochizuki had convinced himself that Yoko would be miserable if she married that man. But who can really predict the future? Had he not disapproved, perhaps now she'd be visiting them regularly, with an adorable grandchild in tow. The thought that it was his actions alone that deprived them of such a joy resided immovably in his mind.

That was when he caught wind of it: a rumor about a café with the power to transport you back in time. It spoke of being able to revisit whichever time you wished to rendezvous with someone you longed to meet.

Absurd.

That was his initial reaction. It was too far-fetched to be real. But as days went by, he became more intrigued.

What if…what if I could truly revisit the past? Could I possibly see my daughter again? Could I right my wrong?

Then, at some point, Mochizuki found himself thinking, *If I could relive that day, this time, I would want to give my blessing instead of objecting…*

Is he really serious about returning to the past?

Kayoko Mochizuki was mulling things over as she

walked home a few steps behind her husband from the café whose basement location made her feel claustrophobic. Unbeknownst to him, she had stayed in contact with Yoko: after she had eloped, she got in touch, sharing her new phone number and new address. But she had made it perfectly clear: "Don't ever let Dad know."

Kayoko had received word from Yoko that she was living happily and harmoniously with her husband, Tetsuya. Although she felt bad for Mochizuki, she had secretly gone to meet their grandchild. But she had not met Tetsuya, not since the day he came to receive approval for the marriage. The timing never matched, as he was always busy with work.

Kayoko had always known that even as a child, Yoko possessed a strong sense of responsibility. In high school, when she joined the judo club for just one month, she did so for a reason. A friend of hers with no judo experience was unsure about joining, so she proposed that they give it a try together. Their agreement was for one month. When the month elapsed, Yoko chose again, to join the wind instrument club, while her friend stayed on with the judo team.

"You left? Didn't I tell you? Judo just isn't for you."

"I was always going to leave after a month."

"That kind of excuse-making won't cut it when you're out in the real world."

"Dad, you never believe in me, do you?"

"We're not talking about that now, are we? I told you I was against it when you said you wanted to join the judo team."

"Enough."

"I've always told you to listen to the end of a conversation!"

Kayoko had always seen Mochizuki and Yoko talking past each other like that. A similar conversation took place when Yoko joined the astronomy club at college.

"Why bother when you're going to give up halfway through anyway?"

"Why do you always assume that?"

"I'm not assuming anything. I know you. I understand you."

"You don't understand anything at all, do you?"

"I do understand. You're bound to give up halfway."

"Okay, then... If I stick with it and don't give up, you'll be happy, right?"

"There's no way you can."

If it's worth belonging to something, then it's worth putting in the effort. So, not wanting to be a member in name alone, Yoko continued to actively participate in the astronomy club throughout college.

Kayoko had wondered if Yoko's true passion would have been to continue with the wind instrument club, but Yoko never complained. She was her mother's pride and joy.

Even when Yoko talked about eloping, Kayoko never tried to stop her, as she had faith that Yoko took ownership of her decisions and actions.

Kayoko thought: *Though we are family, my husband and daughter were constantly at loggerheads. Now that she's grown and has her own family, she doesn't need to conform to her father's life. She's still doing well, living happily with her husband, Tetsuya, and their child in Shizuoka, away from Tokyo. There's no need to interfere. Things are fine as they are.*

So she never once considered letting Mochizuki in on the new chapter in Yoko's life.

Then one day, out of the blue, Mochizuki declared he wanted to visit the café that could take you back in time. Upon hearing this, Kayoko couldn't help but fear that he might return to that pivotal day and once again object to their daughter's marriage.

If he managed to change her mind, it would be catastrophic. It could shatter all the happiness our daughter has found.

Kayoko thought Mochizuki was being obstinate. She suspected that if he managed to travel back, he wouldn't return until he'd worn Yoko down.

Kayoko tentatively accompanied him to the café, but it was soon clear her fears were unfounded. There were many rules to this time-travel business, and they all seemed to favor Yoko. No matter how persuasive Mochizuki might be, he couldn't change the present, and he couldn't stay in the past for long, either. Most importantly, it was not possible to meet anyone who had never been to the café before. On hearing that, Kayoko thought, *I've no idea whether Yoko ever visited this café. Even if he managed to go back, it's more likely he wouldn't get to see her. He must have realized that.*

She felt a wave of relief wash over her. They left the café and headed toward the station.

But then, in that moment, "Mr. Mochizuki!"

The call from behind halted their steps. Turning around, they were met with a woman gasping for air. It was Fumiko Kiyokawa, beads of sweat tracing the contours of her neck and forehead.

"Wait, weren't you...?" Kayoko murmured. The woman was familiar.

Wasn't she in the café, just now? It was dark, and I didn't get a good look, but she knows our name. It must be her.

"Is something wrong?"

Kayoko had stepped in to answer, as Mochizuki appeared stunned upon turning around.

Pouring it all out in one breath, Fumiko said to Mochizuki, "Oh, thank God I caught up with you! Please, head back to the café. Your daughter. She came from the future to meet you!"

"Our daughter?" Mochizuki asked quietly.

Kayoko felt unsettled by how Fumiko had said it.

Fumiko was clearly looking at Mochizuki and Mochizuki alone when she said "your daughter." Kayoko needed some clarification as to whether that was intentional.

"She came to see my husband?"

Fumiko adjusted to a straighter posture. "Yes," she replied with complete certainty.

The station was just ahead. Yet, without hesitation, Mochizuki began walking back with Fumiko. Kayoko trailed a few meters behind them with less certainty.

If what she's saying is true, why would my daughter want to see him? Why not me?

Kayoko's expression darkened.

The sky, too, which had been clear just moments ago, was being overrun by dark rain-filled clouds.

"How did it go?" Kazu Tokita asked Yoko, who had just returned from her trip to the past.

Instead of immediately responding to Kazu's question, Yoko looked around the café. As an underground establishment, it had no windows. Isolated from the sun's light, one must rely on clocks to tell the time. However, the three pendulum wall clocks in the café showed three different times. That made it entirely unclear to Yoko, who was visiting this café for the first time, which clock was showing the right time.

"I guess I've come back from the past, right?"

"Yes," Kazu replied succinctly.

Oh, okay, then…

Yoko had truly managed to journey back to the day her dad, Mochizuki, visited the café. Yet their paths had not crossed. According to Nagare Tokita, clad in his cook's uniform, it was Yoko's deep-rooted reluctance that kept them apart. On reflection, she felt there was some truth to it.

Though I said I wanted to meet him, deep down, I was petrified.

She wondered how it would have gone if they had met.

There, what did I say? You went and married that man, and you became unhappy. You made a mistake. All because you didn't listen to me.

She was quite sure that was how it would have gone.

After Yoko eloped with Tetsuya Kawashima, they left Tokyo and rented an apartment in the city of Shizuoka, a couple of hours away. They vowed to live on their own without relying on anyone else.

At first, things went well. Tetsuya found a new job, and Yoko began part-time work at a convenience store. After a short while, she realized she was pregnant. She was overjoyed, but Tetsuya was not. He was not fond of children.

Almost overnight, his demeanor turned cold. His words grew harsh, and he started to show a violent side.

There were times when he went as far as to kick her stomach, which frightened Yoko terribly. She often considered consulting her mother about the situation but in the end she endured silently, not wanting to worry her.

My mother has been my rock, always standing by my side. I don't want to make her sad. The choice to run away with him was mine, so it's up to me to see it through.

Yoko resolved to leave Tetsuya and raise their unborn child on her own. The moment she broached the subject of their split, Tetsuya signed the divorce papers, as if he had been expecting this all along.

In no time, Tetsuya's new girlfriend showed up at their apartment. Having an affair while his wife was pregnant, Tetsuya turned out to be the worst kind of man. It was then that Yoko understood; her father had seen Tetsuya for the dirtbag he truly was.

I was so blind to it all. I can just imagine how Dad would shake his head at me. And if Mom ever found out about this, it would break her heart.

While she was pregnant, Yoko was fortunate to find a job that offered her room and board, preparing meals for the employees of a newspaper home delivery sales office run by an elderly couple. The pay was low, but it was more important to have a roof over her head and food on the table. The kindly elderly couple were also supportive of the birth, and they took care of various things during her time off.

Yoko kept the divorce a secret from Kayoko, who contacted her every now and then, and falsely reassured her that all was well. Kayoko's longing to see her grandchild led Yoko to arrange a few visits, and not for a moment did Kayoko suspect the truth.

Yoko knew that as her son grew up the lie would inevitably unravel. But she was determined that the truth would only be revealed after she had secured a sufficiently paying job and found an apartment to demonstrate that she and Mitsuru could live a stable life, supporting themselves.

To that end, Yoko worked tirelessly. Although her pay was low, the job at the newspaper sales office was a haven, as it allowed her to work with her child by her side. The elderly couple were happy to care for him while she worked the cash register at a supermarket during her free moments.

Yoko was diligently saving money and was on course to having enough funds to rent an apartment. However, she was fated to repeat the same mistake again.

When Yoko's son turned six, she struck up a friendship

with a man who was a frequent customer at the supermarket where she worked. From their conversations, Yoko learned he was five years older than her and that he worked in property and land consulting.

Yoko did not understand the content of the work at all. All she knew was that it was not a company job, and that it could be done at home with just a computer.

One day, he suggested buying an apartment in the metropolitan area, so that the three of them could live together. It was a proposal she thought worthy of consideration.

We've only known each other for less than six months, but he is really kind, and Mitsuru seems to like him. Also, living in an apartment in the city would give me the confidence to tell both Mom and Dad that I've remarried.

At the moment when the ring was presented to her, Yoko had no reason to say no. She joined him for a viewing of the apartment they were going to buy, leaving the rest of the paperwork to him. She handed over the money she had saved as a down payment, and waited for news that the purchase was complete.

But no matter how long Yoko waited, the call never came. His phone was uncontactable. In desperation, she reached out to the estate agent handling the deal, only to find they had no record of the purchase.

It was a scam. She had been fooled.

Why? Her world had gone completely dark in front of her eyes. *Why must I suffer this way not once, but twice?*

Yoko had already left her jobs at the newspaper sales office and the supermarket, with the expectation of marrying. She had said her goodbyes to the couple who had helped her. She had never imagined that her plan to move into her newly purchased apartment would just evaporate. But it had, leaving her and Mitsuru to face a future filled with uncertainty.

Crushed by despair and without a place to go, Yoko's only remaining choice was to humble herself before her father, confess the truth to her mother, and plead to return home.

For my son's sake. There's no other way, Yoko told herself.

But at the moment she resolved that this was the only course of action and was about to press the call button on her phone, she received a call. It was from Kayoko. The timing was so exact that Yoko's heart pounded, as if she was being watched.

"Hello?"

"Yoko, I've got some bad news."

"What is it?"

"...You see..."

"What's wrong? Are you crying?"

"Your father...away."

"What? You cut out. What about Dad?"

"He's dead."

"What?"

The cause was a sudden hemorrhagic stroke. Mochizuki had collapsed without warning, slipping away into unconsciousness, and that's how he left the world behind.

The last conversation Yoko had with him came flooding back to her.

"I don't think you understand what marriage is. Think about it more carefully, Yoko. That man's no good."

"How can you even tell what kind of person he is?"

"The question is, what do you know about him? You'll be the one to suffer."

"Why did you decide that?"

"You're just too young to be thinking about marriage."

"Oh, stop treating me like a child! If you don't give your blessing, I'll leave this house."

"Suit yourself, then."

"I will, whether you like it or not."

"Don't come crying to me later. Even if you beg, I won't let you back in this house."

"That's fine by me."

Back then, Yoko had been full of defiance. She stormed out of the house and ended up getting burned not once, but twice. And now, just when she was on the verge of collapse and about to seek help, her father died, leaving their anger with each other unresolved.

What must Dad have thought of me?

According to Kayoko, whenever she was even mentioned, her father became tight-lipped and his mood soured.

He must have been so angry he couldn't even bear to talk about it. There's no helping it. After all, I did what I did…

On the night of the funeral, Yoko laid her whole story bare to Kayoko. Kayoko wept and chided her, questioning why she hadn't sought advice sooner. When she explained that she hadn't wanted to cause worry, Kayoko's tears flowed anew. Seeing Yoko with nowhere else to turn, she urged her to come back home: "Let's live together."

Yoko knew she had no other choices, but she couldn't bring herself to accept Kayoko's offer just like that.

"Thank you, but…"

"What's stopping you?"

"What would Dad think…?"

"If your father knew how much you'd been suffering, he'd definitely tell you to come home."

"But…"

The last thing her father said to her was stuck in her ears. "Don't come crying to me later. Even if you beg,

I won't let you back in this house." She just couldn't shake those words.

I've been so selfish. I don't have the right to return home. I'm paying the price for leaving home like that and angering Dad. To say "Okay, I'll move back in" merely because he died is just too convenient. How can I possibly live in his home when I trampled on his wishes?

But when Yoko turned down her mother's proposal, Kayoko suggested something quite odd.

"Well then, why not go back in time and ask your father?"

But Yoko didn't get to see him.

"My time there ended abruptly when I stood up from my seat."

"Is that so?"

Kazu Tokita's face didn't betray a single emotion as she listened to Yoko's explanation. She simply picked up the coffee cup, still almost full.

"I'll brew some fresh hot coffee for you," she whispered before vanishing into the kitchen.

After a moment, the woman in the white dress returned from the toilet. Surrendering her seat to her, Yoko took a seat at the neighboring table.

"Mommy."

While Yoko had been journeying back to the past, her son had been waiting for her at the café. He emerged from the living quarters at the back and rushed over to her.

"Mitsuru, have you been a good boy?"

Instead of answering his mother, Mitsuru held out a skeleton doll dressed as Santa for her to see.

"Where did you get that?"

"She gave it to me."

"Who did?"

Rather than replying, Mitsuru silently looked behind him. Following his gaze, Yoko spotted a woman in her midforties. Her name was Kyoko Kijima, a regular at the café. She, too, had a son, who was in grade four of elementary school. However, the person who gave Mitsuru the doll wasn't Kyoko but a little girl with wide, sparkling eyes standing beside her. The young girl's name was Miki Tokita, Nagare's daughter, who was turning six that year.

"Did you say thank you?" Yoko asked, and Mitsuru gave a small solemn nod.

"You couldn't meet him?"

It was Kyoko who interjected. She was visiting the café and overheard Kazu and Yoko's conversation. Understanding Yoko's predicament, she offered to watch over Mitsuru while Yoko went back to the past.

In truth, Kyoko's younger brother had recently appeared to visit their mother. He had traveled back from a time where she had already died of cancer. So Yoko's need to see her deceased father resonated with her.

"I didn't end up returning to a time when my father was in the café..."

"Oh, that's a shame." Kyoko sighed sympathetically, as if this were her own loss.

"Yes," Yoko replied, gently patting Mitsuru's head as he cradled the doll with care. "But maybe that was how it was meant to be."

"What do you mean by that?" Kyoko asked, her head tilted in curiosity.

"I've just lost all my money and I have no place to live, so I have no other option than to return home. I think going back to asking my father for forgiveness was just for my own peace of mind..."

"But still..."

"It's okay. I'm disappointed, but..." Yoko replied, her words tinged with a hint of guilt.

I'm actually relieved. I'm glad I didn't see Dad. I can't say that, though. But that's what I'm feeling deep down. What a horrible daughter I am.

Yoko's inner voice only amplified her feelings.

Why did I elope in the first place?

Why didn't I tell them after my first failure?

The more she thought, the more her mind sank into an unfathomable darkness. Seeing Yoko so withdrawn, Kyoko also lost her words, and before long, Miki had fallen asleep in Kyoko's arms. She checked the clock: the time had just passed eight in the evening.

There's no point in staying any longer. We should get going.

But just as Yoko took Mitsuru's hand and was about to stand up…

"I apologize for the delay."

It was Kazu Tokita, who had abruptly returned from the kitchen.

"Oh, we were about to…"

"Please…have some coffee while you wait."

Kazu served Yoko coffee and Mitsuru hot milk before disappearing back into the kitchen, leaving Yoko at a loss. She looked over at Kyoko, who had taken a seat at the counter. Kyoko smiled and nodded slightly as if to say: *Well, she's gone to the trouble of serving it—you may as well drink it.*

Yoko sighed and sat back down. Mitsuru was already seated at the table across from her, sipping his milk.

I've failed as a daughter. Maybe I should have reached out when Mitsuru was born. I didn't because I was stubborn. I even made Mom promise not to tell Dad, and because of that, he died without ever seeing his grandson.

Yoko couldn't bring herself to even touch the coffee

that had been set before her. Letting out sighs was all she could do at that moment. Her heart had sunk as dark and deep as the inky black coffee in her cup.

My regret feels so overwhelming. I can never see Dad again. I had my chance, I could have returned to the day when my father came to this café, and I squandered it.

One of the mysterious rules for traveling back in time at this café was that you couldn't meet anyone who hadn't been there before. Her mother had told her, "I believe your father wanted to go back to prevent your marriage. But he learned that he couldn't meet anyone who hadn't visited this café, so he gave up and was going to go home. If you could return to that very moment, you should be able to meet him."

"Wait, what?"

She said he was going to go home. Why didn't she just say he went home?

As Yoko reminisced about her conversation with Kayoko, she felt a nagging sensation that something important was being overlooked.

That was not all.

What did the waitress just say? "Please…have some coffee while you wait."

…who am I supposed to be waiting for?

Yoko had brushed off what Kazu had said as a mere mistake in words, but when taken together with what

Kayoko had said, it now nagged at her. She reached for her coffee in an attempt to soothe her unsettled mind.

That's when it happened.

Initially Yoko thought the wall facing her was blurring into a white haze. Then she realized it was actually the woman in the white dress at the neighboring table morphing into a misty white apparition. It resembled the way a ninja might vanish in a puff of smoke. Yoko instantly recognized what it was from her own experience.

It's like the moment I went back in time.

Immediately after Kazu had served her the coffee, Yoko's body had seemed like it became one with the steam from the coffee cup.

The same thing is happening.

Yoko sensed that someone would emerge from beneath the misty veil.

"He was going to go home."

"Please…have some coffee while you wait."

Her heart racing, Yoko pulled Mitsuru close to her and lifted him onto her lap.

"Ah…"

The white haze that had enveloped the woman in the white dress was sucked into the ceiling, revealing the very person she thought would appear.

"Dad…?"

"Yoko."

It was her father. Upon hearing her name in that raspy, low voice, Yoko stiffened.

Kayoko had returned with Mochizuki to the dimly lit café, which she found claustrophobic.

"So, as you brought me back here, I gather that means I can see my daughter?"

"Exactly!"

Fumiko's eyes sparkled as she answered without hesitation.

Kayoko's face contorted with confusion.

"What are you talking about? You said my daughter came from the future, right? I thought this café allowed you to go back to the past, not travel to the future."

"Well, actually, you can travel to the future, too," Nagare explained.

"What?"

The whole idea of going back to the past seems preposterous enough.

Kayoko, already skeptical, kept her thoughts to herself.

"This café isn't just about going back in time. It allows you to travel to any time you desire."

"Any time I desire?"

"Yes. So you can even go to the future. Though it's seldom a customer chooses to do that."

"Why not?"

"Well, say there's someone you want to meet in the future. Would you know when, exactly, they would be visiting this café?"

"How could I know that…? Oh, I see."

"That's right. If you're going back to the past, all you need to know is the time when the person you want to meet was in this café. But…"

"If it's the future, you can't know?"

"Exactly."

"But because my daughter came from the future…"

"It means that if you were to travel to the future targeting the exact time your daughter was here, you could meet her."

"But if our daughter was here just a moment ago, why go all the way to the future when it's possible to just go back a few minutes from now?"

"Oh… I didn't think of that."

Fumiko slapped her hand, realizing a blind spot in her reasoning, and looked at Nagare.

"But that's not possible."

"Why not?"

The one who persisted in exacting the facts was Fumiko.

Kayoko, who posed the question, was observing the exchange between Nagare and Fumiko with a cool expression.

"Because there is only one seat."

"...Ah, I see."

Satisfied, Fumiko's fervor suddenly cooled.

"I'm sorry. I don't follow." Kayoko looked confused.

"The seat your husband would need to be in would already be occupied by your daughter visiting from the future."

"So that's why... Oh." Finally grasping the situation, Kayoko stopped her objection midway.

"That's just how it is. Two people can't return to the same time. There is only one chair," Nagare clarified.

"Is that so? I see," Kayoko said, apparently finding Nagare's explanation satisfactory. However, in her mind, she mused,

If my husband's aim is to make Yoko cancel her marriage by going back in time, then what's the point in traveling to the future?

"What are you thinking, honey?"

Mochizuki ignored Kayoko as he stared at the time-traveling chair, in which the woman in the white dress was seated. Anyone planning to venture through time must first wait for her to leave it to go to the toilet.

Nagare picked up where he left off. "Your daughter

mentioned she came from four years into the future. But I don't know the exact time."

"I do," Fumiko said, raising her hand.

"Really?"

The surprised response belonged to Nagare.

"Yes, I actually know the time."

"How could you know that?"

"I saw what time it was on her watch," Fumiko said, tapping on her left wrist.

"You know how a lot of women wear their watches with the face on the inside of the wrist? Well, she had hers on the outside. That caught my eye, so I looked closer. It was digital, and it said 6:45 p.m. It also displayed the date, which was the 11th of November. No question about it," Fumiko declared confidently.

"So, it's 6:45 p.m. on the 11th of November, four years from now. Perfect. We know everything we need to know." Nagare gave a thumbs-up to Fumiko, impressed by her keen observation. "So, what do you wish to do?"

Knowing all facts needed to reach the destination, Nagare had now turned to Mochizuki.

But Kayoko had reservations.

Why would he go to the future? Going there won't help him accomplish whatever he's trying to do. If he just wants to meet her, he can just visit this café again in four years.

Speaking for her silent husband, Kayoko started to decline.

"I regret to inform you that my husband was planning to travel back to the past, to see our daughter before she got married..." However, Mochizuki silenced her with a simple hand gesture. "...What?"

Ignoring his wife's look of surprise, Mochizuki lowered his head and pleaded, "Please, let me go to the future. To the future where my daughter will be."

However...

How long are they going to keep me waiting?

Three hours had passed since Mochizuki decided to travel to the future. Kayoko had gone home, mentioning that she had to prepare dinner. The pendulum clocks on the wall of the café all showed different times, making them useless. Mochizuki checked his watch. 7:20 p.m. There were no windows, but he was sure it must be dark outside by now. While waiting, he had consumed two cups of coffee. He had naively thought he'd be back in time for dinner, but now his stomach was protesting that assumption.

They said she was a ghost, but...

Mochizuki took another look at the woman in the

white dress. Sitting motionless and engrossed in a book, she was wearing a short-sleeved dress despite it being a little early to be wearing something for the peak of summer. He and that woman were the only customers present. Behind the counter were Kazu and Nagare. Nagare was holding his daughter Miki, who was quietly sleeping. She had just turned two this year. Nagare's wife, Kei, had passed away shortly after Miki was born.

"As a parent myself, I can imagine the sorrow she felt not being able to see her own child grow up," Mochizuki had told Nagare, his heart aching for him.

Then Nagare said, with his already thin eyes narrowing even more, "Actually, my wife also went to the future—to see our daughter when she had grown to be in junior high school." His eyes seemed almost to smile as he spoke.

"Incredible…"

Mochizuki was riveted by Nagare's tale.

"So, she got to meet her?"

"Yes. Thanks to that, my wife was able to pass away with a smile. She never told me what they talked about, though," Nagare said, his eyes shifting to a framed photograph of Kei on the counter. Mochizuki thought she had a captivating smile.

"In my case… I don't have high hopes that the story of me and my daughter will have as happy an ending, even if I go to the future and meet her. I had hoped I could go back in time. I was considering giving my blessing for her marriage, you see. Even if that wouldn't change the reality of her eloping, at least if I were to give my approval, in the future, she might come back if she ever faces hardships. Or perhaps I could offer her some advice, too."

Mochizuki began to mutter as if speaking to himself.

"That's how I was thinking. But I have to rethink things if I am traveling to four years into the future. I don't think it would mean much to her if I said anything like that. I bet she hasn't forgiven me for objecting to her marriage. The fact that she hasn't sent so much as a text since then is evidence enough of that."

Lowering his eyes, Mochizuki let out a quiet sigh.

"So, why did you even consider going back to the past?" Nagare asked with an inquisitive tilt of the head.

"Well…"

Mochizuki began to share, in scattered words, why he had contemplated traveling back in time.

One night at dinner, he'd suddenly asked Kayoko, "Do you remember Yoko's favorite dish?"

It was just one of those questions that popped out, no special reason behind it.

"What's with the sudden question?"

It was understandable for Kayoko to be startled. Yoko was a taboo subject between them after she had eloped.

She doesn't ever mention it, but Kayoko probably blames me for Yoko leaving.

That's how Mochizuki saw it.

Kayoko's mood always soured noticeably whenever Mochizuki brought up their daughter.

"Yes, her favorite dish."

He had already asked, so it was pointless to retract his question.

"If I remember right, it's omurice."

Why is he bringing this up out of the blue? Kayoko's thought could be fathomed from the crease between her eyebrows.

"Oh, I see."

"What?"

"Nothing important."

But this was not a trivial matter at all. As he answered, Mochizuki had a moment of stunned clarity.

Did I really say no to my daughter's marriage without even knowing what her favorite food is?

Sure, it was ridiculous to place taste in food on the same level as a marriage partner. But that notion unsettled him, nevertheless.

What did I know about Yoko's life? She has her own tastes, her own experiences. I shouldn't have tried to guide her all the time. At some point, she would have had to make big life choices without me. And when we choose our way in life, sometimes we mess up… It's simply impossible to always be there to help. Protection is not everything. It would have been better if I let her gain the strength to overcome adversity by herself. In wishing for Yoko's happiness, perhaps I've inadvertently narrowed her choices.

It was only then that Mochizuki finally understood that he had been wrong to oppose his daughter's marriage.

"Maybe I should've trusted her choices and waited. That way at least she would feel she could always come home. Back in the day, I was just pushing my own agenda. I wasn't genuinely looking out for her happiness. At the very least, I want to say I'm sorry for that. That's where my heart is now."

With life comes many regretful actions that we can't undo. Most of these come down to things we do or say in the heat of the moment. Fallouts that occur in a family—among parent and child, or among siblings—can take a long time to resolve. No amount of regret over past words and actions can heal the emotional wounds inflicted on someone unless that person's feelings change.

Mochizuki's words flowed quietly into Kazu's listening ears, while Nagare murmured, "Is that so…" and narrowed his eyes even further.

Flap.

The sudden sound of a book snapping shut reverberated through the café. Mochizuki turned to see the woman in the white dress slowly rising from her seat.

"She got up!" Mochizuki blurted inadvertently before clamping his mouth shut in embarrassment. But the woman in the white dress took no notice of him as she silently made her way past his table, her footsteps entirely inaudible, and exited the door to the toilet.

Mochizuki looked over as if to say, *What should I do?*

Kazu Tokita, who had been silent up to this point, said, "Please, have a seat and wait here," before vanishing into the kitchen.

Taking Nagare's nod as a cue, Mochizuki got up and stood beside the chair.

At last I'll get to see Yoko. But Kayoko must be puzzling over why I'd want to venture into the future. She's probably finished making dinner by now and getting annoyed that I'm still not home.

Mochizuki had heard Kayoko sigh softly as she was leaving the café. Overriding such concerns, though, was one fact: *Yoko actually came to see me.*

Had she not, he might never have considered making this trip into the future. *Maybe when I see her, she'll forgive me.*

This flicker of hope was also feeding his thoughts.

Summoning his resolve, Mochizuki slid into the chair left vacant by the woman in the white dress.

Once seated, he became aware of a subtle coolness enveloping the space around the chair. Reaching out to explore this phenomenon, he sensed a temperature boundary just a few inches from his fingertips.

It's not that the chair itself is cold, but rather, this space has a different temperature altogether.

Mochizuki had an undeniable feeling that he was in a special, time-traveling space.

"Sorry to keep you waiting."

Kazu reappeared from the kitchen, carrying a tray with a pristine white coffee cup and a silver kettle. What would unfold from here was something Mochizuki couldn't begin to fathom. Picking up on his puzzled expression, Kazu began her explanation.

"I will now serve you a cup of coffee… Your planned destination is four years into the future, is that correct?"

"Yes," Mochizuki confirmed, stealing a quick glance at Nagare, who nodded back.

"Very well. Your journey to the future will begin once I pour coffee into this cup…" While speaking, Kazu set a pristine white coffee cup in front of Mochizuki.

"And it will last only until the coffee becomes completely cold."

"Until it gets cold? Is that all the time I have?"

"Yes."

"I see…"

Mochizuki had heard there was a time limit, but it was shorter than he'd ever imagined.

He had sipped his way through a few cups of coffee while waiting for the woman in the white dress to pay a visit to the toilet. And something had caught his attention about the coffees served at this café. They were a bit cooler than in other establishments. The upcoming brew might be special from the others and served hotter. But if it was a bit cooler like the others, the time needed for it to go cold could hardly be more than ten minutes—perhaps just seven or eight minutes, or even less. That thought nagged at him. Given the brief time available, would he have time to really convey his feelings to Yoko, the daughter he had not seen in years?

Mochizuki's face crinkled with anxiety as he said, "All right."

"Once you are in the future, be sure to drink up your entire cup of coffee before it goes cold."

How many more of these tedious rules are there?

Mochizuki felt a flicker of annoyance as he was introduced to yet another rule.

"What if I don't finish the coffee?" His words, though not intentionally so, were tinged with irritation.

Unperturbed, Kazu answered with an equanimous expression.

"If you don't finish it, you'll be the one who remains seated in that chair."

"Me?"

"Yes."

Lost for words, Mochizuki fell silent. Kazu's single-sentence reply carried a gravitas that left him speechless. It was clear she was not joking.

Ah, I see, Mochizuki mused. Of course, there would be risks involved in traveling through time. It somehow made sense. Miracles came with risks, after all.

"Understood," he said.

Kazu, reading his expression, decided that no further clarification was needed on that rule and returned to explaining the procedure for traveling to the future.

"There is one thing that you must remember," she said emphatically.

"What's that?"

"Whatever facts you learn in the future cannot be changed, no matter how hard you try after you return. That's the rule. It's absolute."

"Er, all right," Mochizuki responded, although he couldn't fully grasp the implications of what he'd just been told.

In his mind, while the past was set in stone, and therefore could not be changed, the future was still in flux and so he was assuming that there would be no limits on his actions when going forward.

"For instance," she continued, "imagine you go to the future and find out your car will be stolen in a week. Despite knowing this, you can do nothing to change that fact."

"Why? If I know it's going to be stolen, I can prevent it— Ah!" At that moment, he understood what she was trying to say.

It was the crux—or perhaps the pitfall—of the rule that "no matter how hard you try to change things after traveling through time, reality remains the same."

Carefully, Mochizuki attempted to put his newfound understanding into words.

"Am I right in understanding that this rule is not about what will happen, but about what I've come to know will happen?"

"Exactly," Kazu replied, looking him squarely in the eye.

Mochizuki quickly organized the thoughts swirling in his head.

If, for instance, he went to the future and found out his car would be stolen, he could take any measures to prevent that event—hide the car, hire security, and so on. In other words, his actions leading up to the event could change because of his future knowledge. However, even if his actions could change, the fact that the car would be stolen cannot be altered, no matter what he did.

"I see."

As Mochizuki touched on the crux of this rule, he felt his heart waver by the risk of a fate of despair, sealed by a future he could not change, no matter how hard he tried.

"Shall we proceed?" Kazu asked softly, her hand poised over the kettle that sat on the tray before her.

No matter what he learned from venturing into the future, those facts would be unchangeable. Even if he discovered his daughter, Yoko, to be unhappy, he could do nothing to alleviate her suffering. He would have to go on living knowing that helplessness.

"Are you ready?" Kazu asked. This was his last chance to opt out.

Should I really do this? He could be condemning himself to four years of mental anguish.

Still, Yoko—my long-estranged daughter—chose to come to see me. She must have a compelling reason. If I don't go, she may never get another chance to see me. No need for indecision.

Mochizuki's mind was made up.

"Please proceed," he said, locking eyes with Kazu, whose hand was still poised above the silver kettle.

"Very well, then…" Kazu straightened her back, inhaled, and whispered, "Before the coffee gets cold."

At that moment, a palpable tension filled the café.

Slowly, Kazu lifted the silver kettle from the tray and began elegantly pouring coffee into the cup. She executed this ordinary action with the graceful beauty of a ballerina.

Uh…

A wisp of steam rose from the cup, now filled to the brim. Mochizuki followed its ascent with his eyes. Although he was certain he was following the steam, his perspective inexplicably began to rise toward the ceiling. The scene around him seemed to be flowing from top to bottom, until he himself had become an ethereal wisp.

Oh!

As his surroundings morphed more and more rapidly, his consciousness began dissipating. Amid the fading awareness, he found himself reminiscing about the time he had first met his wife.

"You made the worst first impression," Kayoko told Mochizuki when he proposed to her.

She was referring to her orientation period at a company they both worked for when she was still learning the ropes. Mochizuki had approached her.

"Hey, if you don't have any tasks, speak up. Do you

intend to get paid just for standing there?" he had said gruffly.

"Oh, sorry."

"If you don't have any tasks, speak up."

Reflecting on that time, Kayoko said, "I was scared of you… I had finished all the work assigned to me, and I wanted to ask why I was being reprimanded. But I didn't dare speak up, thinking it would only provoke you more. At that moment, I felt hopeless, thinking I'd have to work under such a boss for the rest of my life. I never would have thought that you'd end up proposing to me."

Confronted by Kayoko's laughter, Mochizuki showed discomfort. He never intended to intimidate her. It was actually quite the opposite. He admired how diligently Kayoko had followed his instructions.

"Hey, you."

Hey, you, whatever your name is.

"If you have no work, say so."

Have you already finished your work?

"Do you intend to get paid just for standing there?"

If you have free time, could you help me with my work?

The truth was, the words Mochizuki had thrown at Kayoko were far removed from what he actually wanted to say.

Nevertheless, no matter what Mochizuki had intended, being on the receiving end was anything but easy. Previous newcomers had been similarly subjected to Mochizuki's demeanor; some avoided him, while others even decided to leave. To the new hires just entering the workforce, the true intent behind Mochizuki's words was often lost.

In their unseasoned eyes, Mochizuki might have seemed like an unreasonable boss. But in reality, his sense of responsibility was second to none, and he was genuinely kind at heart. So those who truly knew him rated him highly.

The problem was his far-from-diplomatic choice of words. Discerning his true intentions was a monumental task if one only had a brief interaction with him.

However, Kayoko did not run away. Although intimidated, she faced Mochizuki squarely. Mochizuki, too, had respect for the way Kayoko handled her work. Over time, that respect changed into affection.

For Kayoko as well, Mochizuki evolved into a person who might be bad with words but was genuinely kind and trustworthy.

"If the me from back then heard this, she'd strongly object," Kayoko prefaced before accepting Mochizuki's marriage proposal.

Three years later, Yoko was born.

"Yoko."

Yoko's heartbeat raced at the sound of her name. As expected, it was her father, Mochizuki, occupying the time-traveling seat. On the night of the funeral, Kayoko had mentioned he "was going to go home."

So, Dad did return to this café on that day.

Mochizuki, the man she had avoided meeting even once since she had eloped, was now right before her eyes.

"Mommy?"

Startled by her son Mitsuru's voice, she came back to her senses. She noticed that Mochizuki's gaze was also locked on to Mitsuru.

Is he your son?

Her father's eyes were wide open in astonishment. His surprise was understandable. He had suddenly come face-to-face with his six-year-old grandson.

"Yes, this is Mitsuru."

"I see."

She noticed that even though he didn't speak the words, Mochizuki's lips minutely moved as if silently mouthing the name Mitsuru. Gazing at Mitsuru, his eyes became kinder.

"It's a good name, isn't it?" She felt her voice tremble as she spoke.

"Yes."

I'm glad I was able to introduce my son.

When she learned of Mochizuki's death, Yoko felt burdened by two regrets: her decision to elope, and her failure to ever introduce her son to him.

She had kept in touch with Kayoko, even arranging occasional visits. Mitsuru had come to call her "Grandma," and the relationship between them was warm.

Mom never said it, but I know she must have wished that Dad and I would make up.

Yoko realized that her stubbornness had prevented that, partly because she never thought her father would pass away so soon.

Mitsuru's round eyes darted here and there as he examined his grandpa's face.

"Say hello," Yoko urged.

Obliging, Mitsuru gazed up at Mochizuki's stern face and softly said, "Hello."

Mochizuki's already stern face seemed to harden even more, perhaps due to extreme emotional upheaval. Yoko remembered all the times she had felt bewildered and even repelled by that very expression.

But Dad is no longer a part of my life.

The realization that she would never see him again

brought tears to Yoko's eyes. Despite their conflicts and disagreements, a father was still a father, as far as she was concerned.

"Dad," she said with all the courage she could muster.

If I don't tell him about my situation now, I'll regret it. Dad was right to oppose my decision. I should have listened to him. I have nowhere to go now. I must apologize for leaving on my own. I'll tell him I'm sorry and unless he forgives me, I have no right to return home.

"Dad, you see..."

But as the moment came to say those words, her voice failed her. Despite having her deceased father right before her, she couldn't look him in the eye.

"Are you happy?"

"What?"

Yoko looked up at the sound of Mochizuki's muffled voice. His eyes were averted, staring down at the pristine white cup. For a moment, she wasn't even sure it was he who spoke.

Did I hear that right?

Still not completely sure whether the voice she heard was indeed her father's, Yoko answered hesitantly, "Er, yes."

Why am I lying? I'm not happy at all right now. I got divorced, fell for a marriage scam, and I have neither money nor a place to live!

Yet she didn't say that.

"I see," Mochizuki uttered emotionlessly, as if letting out a sigh. Perhaps he found no joy in hearing his daughter, whose marriage he had opposed, claim to be happy.

But the reality was different.

Just as Mochizuki had worried, Yoko was at the depths of unhappiness at this point in her life.

How many minutes have already passed since Dad appeared? Two or three? I can't trust my own perception; I should assume at least five minutes. When I returned to the past earlier and touched the cup, I realized how much it had cooled—it may not even take ten minutes for it to get cold.

Yoko looked up at her father.

"Dad, you see..."

"I was wrong, Yoko."

For a moment, Yoko doubted her ears. But no, those were unmistakably Mochizuki's words.

"I've regretted it for so long."

"Oh, Dad..."

"I'm sorry," Mochizuki said and bowed his head deeply.

"Dad, no." Perhaps Yoko's voice was too soft; her father remained bowed. "Please, lift your head."

Dad wasn't wrong about anything. I was the one who was mistaken. If anyone is apologizing, it should be me.

"You see, actually..."

Mochizuki lifted his face. His eyes darted around nervously. He glanced at his coffee cup, blinked several times, and though he seemed to catch Yoko out of the corner of his eye, he couldn't bring himself to look at her directly.

"I've got something I need to get off my chest, Dad."

As she talked, Yoko's thoughts were a jumbled mess.

I never thought Dad would be living with regret. Mom never mentioned anything like this, either. I thought he passed away without ever forgiving me.

"So, um..."

Her words once again got stuck, and the room seemed to freeze. All the while, the coffee was getting colder.

"Grandpa," Mitsuru suddenly whispered, latching on to Mochizuki's knee. Caught off guard, Mochizuki's eyes widened. He seemed to say, *Grandpa? Does he recognize me?*

"Mom showed him your picture on her phone and said that it was Grandpa."

Truth be told, I never liked the idea of teaching him to call the man in the picture "Grandpa," but I never had the courage to tell Mom to stop.

Now, however, Yoko was seeing everything differently. She had never imagined a moment like this.

"Since we're finally together, how about a hug from Grandpa?" Yoko said, lifting Mitsuru onto Mochizuki's lap. Mitsuru settled without protest. Always an outgoing child, he looked up, waiting for Mochizuki's reaction.

"He's your first grandchild."

(This is the last chance my dad will have to hold him.)

Yoko fought back tears that threatened to spill.

For a moment, Mochizuki froze. Then he cradled Mitsuru's hand in his own and whispered, "My first grandchild."

Mochizuki's face relaxed. The sight caused tears to further well up in Yoko's eyes. She couldn't let them out. As she looked up at the ceiling to compose herself, Mochizuki broke the silence.

"If I had stopped you from marrying, this little one wouldn't be here. I was wrong. I'm sorry."

But while bowing his head, inside he thought, *Thank goodness.*

Because of one rule in this unique café, that reality cannot be altered when traveling to the future no matter how hard you try, once you know something it becomes set in stone. That meant that now Mochizuki knew he had a grandson, that fact would not change.

How truly wonderful. I'm grateful. Now, when I return to my present, I can live on knowing that my daughter is happy, and my grandchild exists.

Mochizuki silently thanked the rules of this otherworldly café.

"Dad…"

Seeing her father bow, Yoko quickly turned away.

Tears were spilling from her eyes, and she found it impossible not to shake from her sobbing.

Why didn't I go back home while Dad was still around? Why could I understand something so important only after it was too late to see him again? How selfish and flawed a daughter am I? What a terrible child I've been to my parents.

Her emotions were a tangled web of regret and self-blame. From behind her, she heard her son's querying voice.

"Grandpa? What's wrong, Grandpa?"

She didn't have to look to know what was happening. Her father was crying, too.

Meeting my deceased father shouldn't even be possible. If I miss this chance, I'll never see him again. Then isn't there something more important I should say right now, beyond apologizing or talking about my life as it is?

Yoko glanced at the pristine white coffee cup placed in front of Mochizuki. Suddenly, the ticking of the wall clock seemed unbearably loud. She had stood up before her coffee had a chance to fully cool, but it had already been seven or eight minutes since Mochizuki had appeared. The more time slipped away, the cooler his untouched coffee would become. There was no stopping it. Time was running out, and her parting moment with Mochizuki was drawing near.

"Ah, yes, I know what I want to say."

Yoko wiped her tears and sniffled, then faced Mochizuki, who was also quickly wiping his eyes.

"I had something important I needed to say to you, Dad."

"Hmm?" Mochizuki responded. He kept his eyes lowered as though he was talking to his grandson.

"I never got the chance to say it because I eloped, remember?"

"Say what?"

"You know that traditional thing daughters say to their fathers on the eve of their wedding..."

Before she could finish her sentence, Mochizuki seemed to choke, his body trembling.

"Don't be silly. Why bring it up now?" The loudness of Mochizuki's voice startled his grandson.

Yet Yoko was unfazed.

"Let me say it."

"No, stop it."

"Let me say this, please. It's my one and only chance," Yoko implored. *I'll never get an opportunity to speak with you again.*

Once more, Yoko's eyes spilled over with tears. Mochizuki briefly met her eyes before looking away. Without a word, he gently eased Mitsuru off his lap. Mitsuru gave his grandfather a quick, inquisitive look before dashing back to his mother. Mochizuki's brow wrinkled, as if concentrating, and he turned an ear toward her.

All right, I'll listen.

Taking Mochizuki's silent cue, Yoko gave a small nod.

"Dad, I know I've been a handful and I'm really sorry. But I'm on the path to happiness. You can stop worrying about me now."

She took a step closer to Mochizuki, and, locking her tear-filled eyes with his, she said softly, "Thank you for looking after me until now. It's been an honor to be your daughter," and gave him a respectful nod.

In response to her words, Mochizuki simply muttered, "Silly girl."

Yoko didn't remember much of what happened after that.

I remember the waitress calling out to Dad, and he gulped down his coffee and returned to the past. Then, with Mitsuru patting my head, I was on my knees crying for a while.

Yoko then went home, and once again, she paid her respects to Mochizuki's memorial photo. "I will be happy," she vowed.

On that day four years earlier, after returning home from the café, Mochizuki pulled out the family photo album which contained photos of Yoko.

Even when Kayoko asked Mochizuki what had happened, he wouldn't tell her anything. However, Kayoko thought that he probably did get to meet Yoko.

No. Not probably. He definitely did meet her. She could tell because seeing her husband smile so joyously while looking at his daughter's photos was something she hadn't witnessed in a long time.

"Honey," Kayoko called out to Mochizuki, who was engrossed in the photos from the adjacent dining kitchen. "Omurice for dinner tonight."

"Omurice?" Pausing his flipping through the album, Mochizuki stared at the photo in his hands and said, "All right, coming now."

In the photo, Yoko was also smiling.

iv

The Valentine

"If only I had superpowers."

Who hasn't dreamed of that?

There are various forms of supernatural powers: telepathy, clairvoyance, ESP, telekinesis, levitation, thoughtography, and psychic healing, to name a few. Back in the late 1980s, TV shows in Japan were obsessed with such powers. On any given night, children and adults alike would tune in to a program showcasing someone with an inexplicable ability, like bending spoons or moving objects without touching them.

The most popular were the clairvoyants, who could see through things—hidden patterns on cards or the contents of envelopes or boxes—or in some cases know about a person's past or secrets simply by looking at them. But there were many shows that exposed trickery. Clairvoyants were accused of having collaborators;

spoon bending was the result of metal fatigue or some other physical principle. There were many confrontations between people exhibiting their abilities and those trying to debunk them.

Everyone will encounter a time when they're unable to say "I love you." But what if you really could read someone's mind? The fear of rejection would be a thing of the past. The biggest obstacle to confessing your love is not knowing what your romantic interest is feeling—it would take some kind of superpower. And feelings are fickle; they change daily. If the timing of a confession is even slightly off, the opportunity may be missed.

This is a story about such a missed opportunity, about a girl who just couldn't break through her own shyness to express how she felt.

I couldn't do it…

Tsumugi Ito let out a heavy sigh as she looked out of her second-floor classroom window at Hayato Nanase walking home from school. Clasped in her hand was a box adorned with a cute ribbon.

"Got cold feet? Missed your once-a-year chance, I see…" Ayame Matsubara loomed ominously behind her. She knew exactly what she was seeing. Ayame had big eyes with long, curled eyelashes, and unlike Tsumugi, who was perpetually tanned, she maintained a translucent porcelain complexion, despite taking part in the same outdoor swimming club activities as Tsumugi.

"Ayame, you don't need to rub it in."

Tsumugi's expression was twisted into regret.

It was the 14th of February, Valentine's Day. In Japan, this is the one day each year when women express their feelings to men with the gift of chocolate. Recipients return the favor one month later on White Day.

The tradition of Valentine's Day dates back to third-century Rome. The emperor had forbidden his soldiers to marry, as he believed they would desert rather than leave their loved ones. A kindhearted priest named Valentine felt sympathy for them, and secretly officiated at their weddings. When the emperor caught wind of this, he was livid. He warned Valentine, but the priest, championing love, resisted. His defiance cost him his life. As time passed, people honored Valentine's courage, naming the day of his execution "Saint Valentine's Day."

Furthermore, according to the old lunar calendar, the 14th of February marked the beginning of spring, a season when birds choose their mates. Therefore, there's a theory suggesting that it grew to be a day to confess one's love, eventually becoming known as a "Day of Lovers," when proposals or gifts were given.

"Oh, cry not, fair maiden, lest your pretty face be spoiled."

"Pray do not with honeyed words seek to soothe me."

"Dost thou accuse me of offering naught but hollow solace? Best wipe your tears with this."

Ayame handed Tsumugi a pale blue handkerchief.

"Much obliged."

Their conversation was always like this, filled with the types of expressions you would hear in Japanese period dramas.

"How pitiful you are. Despite harboring warm affections, you chose not to bestow the gift."

"Please spare me such commentary. It will serve only to bring on more tears."

If only I were as pretty as you, Ayame.

Tsumugi sighed secretly within.

Everyone falls for someone at least once and feels that emotion called love. A first crush during adolescence, in particular, can be so pure and yet so fleeting. Looking back, it may not be entirely clear why you actually fell for that person.

So, why do we fall in love?

There's a theory that it's programmed in our DNA to ensure the continuation of our species. But love is a more intricate emotion that cannot be explained by this theory alone. Something standing out as particularly unnecessary from the point of view of producing offspring, for instance, would be the torment endured by Tsumugi from being unable to express her feelings to the person she had fallen for.

Even if someone were to claim, "It's to stop the population from exploding," that, too, would oversimplify the emotion and rob it of its magic.

Expressing your feelings honestly isn't wrong. It's rare for someone to take offense at being told they are liked—on the contrary, it's a blessing. So why is it so hard to take that step? Saying "I like you" should be simple, but around each person's heart there appears to be a massive wall. Not a physical barrier but an emotional one. When we interact with each other, we hold back because we don't know what's on the other side of the wall.

As humans, we are wired to fear the unknown, and this causes many to falter. But what really is behind that wall? It's the emotions, feelings hidden and unseen, of the other, who may or may not reciprocate. If people could glimpse beyond each other's fortress, and understand their emotions, perhaps, then, they might knock down their wall. Essentially, it is the fear of rejection that makes the wall, and heartbreaks only make it higher.

Tsumugi carried a painful memory. She confessed her feelings to a boy in junior high school (not Hayato), but he replied, "I'm sorry, Tsumugi, but I actually like Ayame."

He was her classmate, and among the male students, her best friend. Their classmates had even teased them, "Why don't you two date?" Tsumugi had been warming up to that idea. But she wasn't in his sights, romantically.

She told Ayame what happened, but couldn't bring herself to tell her why.

Ayame sighed frustratedly and retorted, "What kind of fool would turn down Tsumugi?"

The reason Tsumugi couldn't give chocolates to Hayato Nanase on their final high-school Valentine's Day was the ghost of that painful memory.

If Hayato tells me the same thing, I might not be able to pull through.

Ultimately, the chocolates she prepared never found their way to him; they ended up as a treat for her father instead.

"Do you have a thing for castles?"

Tsumugi still recalled the first words Ayame had said to her.

Ayame was new to the school, transferring just before the summer holidays in the first year of junior high. That day, during break, Tsumugi was engrossed in a castle guidebook she'd finally managed to get. Hearing Ayame's voice from behind all of a sudden caught her off guard.

"Oh, I'm not that into them..." she lied impulsively.

Ayame was stunning. Rumor had it that ten boys asked to go out with her on her very first day. When Tsumugi was approached by someone so beautiful she seemed to come from a manga, she was at a loss for words.

To properly understand how she felt, picture this: you, from a regular background, are out for a stroll in your neighborhood. Not planning to go far, you didn't bother to change out of your casual gray hoodie with matching tracksuit bottoms and sandals. Then suddenly a sleek Porsche pulls up beside you, and out steps a glamorous Hollywood star. It feels surreal. Then out of the blue, she comments, "Nice sandals."

It would seem more real if she scoffed, "Your outfit looks so dull." But no, she's admiring your sandals. How do you even respond to a Hollywood star like that? "They're super-comfy. Want to give them a try?"—that would be unthinkable. Likewise, if you were to tell the star, "I bet they'd look good on you," how audacious would that sound?

Essentially, Tsumugi was dazzled by Ayame's radiant, seemingly otherworldly beauty.

Yet, into her ear, that very same Ayame whispered, "I'm really fond of Takeda Castle."

"Huh?" was the extent to which Tsumugi could respond.

"Takeda Castle. You do know it, don't you?"

Tsumugi's heart leaped at Ayame's words.

"The Castle in the Sky!"

She wasn't talking about the castle in the Studio Ghibli animation Laputa. Takeda Castle, built at the top of a mountain about 350 meters high in Hyogo Prefecture, is also known as Crouching Tiger Castle because the entire mountain resembles a crouching tiger. Nowadays, in this area, dense fog often develops on clear autumn mornings. It surrounds the ruins of Takeda Castle and makes it appear as though it is floating on a sea of clouds. Due to this ethereal sight, the ruins have come to be called "The Castle in the Sky."

So while most people would think of Laputa upon mentioning The Castle in the Sky, if Tsumugi the castle geek heard the name, she would assume the conversation was about Takeda Castle.

"When it was first constructed, it was surrounded by an earthen wall for fortification, but later, this outer wall was converted to stone. That happened during Akamatsu Hirohide's time, didn't it? Hirohide really did a great job, yes?"

Tsumugi was delighted by Ayame's knowledge.

"I, er...really like Kumamoto Castle."

"The daimyo Kato Kiyomasa built that, didn't he? Are you a fan of Kiyomasa?"

"No, I like how the castle is shaped. The stone walls are my favorite part. When I look at the curved construction of the stone and think that Kiyomasa specially hired the Anoshu stonemasons from Omi Province, it just gives me shivers. What could beat that?"

"It has intruder spikes at the top, right? Wow, you're the first girl I've met who gets shivers talking about looking at stone walls."

"I also like the plover-style gables of Kumamoto Castle."

"I love castle gables, too! My favorites are those on Himeji Castle."

"Oh, I agree. Himeji Castle's gables are so pretty. But I still prefer those on Kumamoto Castle."

Tsumugi felt elated. Never before had she met anyone who shared her love for history and castles. It felt like discovering the Hollywood star was wearing the same sandals. An instant bond was established between them, and from that day forward, Ayame became Tsumugi's best friend.

After junior high, Tsumugi and Ayame went to the same high school. By coincidence, they were always in the same class. Ayame believed it was destiny, while Tsumugi thought it was just pure luck.

It was in high school when the two began talking to each other in the samurai tongue. One day, Tsumugi forgot to bring her lunch and was at a loss. Upon learning this, Ayame sighed, "We must share, then," and they shared her lunch.

Gratefully, Tsumugi bowed and said, "Your kindness leaves me deeply in your debt."

This was the spark that ignited their fondness for speaking like samurai with each other. They laughed heartily in a corner of the classroom. Tsumugi didn't recall what they found so funny, but she cherished the memory of sharing laughter over something trivial with a friend. Two history buffs and castle enthusiasts, sharing their unique world through the language of the samurai.

Valentine's Day passed, and in the blink of an eye, the graduation ceremony arrived. The two girls, who had decided on the same university, visited the café Funiculi Funicula in Jimbocho after the ceremony. The only other customer was a woman in a white dress seated at the table in the far corner.

"Forgive my tardiness. Here is your salted caramel roasted green tea latte."

The waitress addressing them in this peculiar manner had big round eyes.

Her name was Kei Tokita. She enjoyed imitating the samurai language used by Tsumugi and Ayame, who frequently visited the café. She had taken a particular liking to this quirky jargon, even using it in her interactions with other customers, much to Nagare's dismay.

"Much obliged," Ayame responded.

"Pray, take thine ease and pass thy time in leisure." Kei bowed with a smile and retreated to the kitchen.

"Verily, I have little stomach for these graduation rites," sighed Tsumugi as she poked a straw into her salted caramel roasted green tea latte. "I've no understanding for everyone's sorrowful visages, parting as if never to meet again. If one hath the will to meet, can it not be arranged at any time?"

"Indeed, thy tongue speaks truth. If thou ever hast the will to see Hayato, could it not be arranged at any moment?" responded Ayame.

Tsumugi clutched her chest and made a face. It had not escaped Ayame's attention that ever since that particular day, Tsumugi would sigh every time she caught sight of Hayato.

"Do not speak of Hayato. That wound has not yet healed," Tsumugi cautioned her.

"My apologies," Ayame replied with a grin.

"More importantly..."

"Hmm?"

"Tell me, why hast thou spurned thy chance to enter the halls of Tokyo University?"

Ayame remained silent for some moments, staring at her caramel green tea latte.

Ayame had always ranked at the top of their class academically. Tsumugi's grades were not bad, but they weren't enough to secure her a place at the University of Tokyo.

"Surely the reason is obvious."

"Then pray tell."

"To share the same university halls as thee," Ayame said with a straight face.

"What?"

Tsumugi couldn't decipher whether Ayame was joking or serious. And if Ayame was serious, she couldn't comprehend why she would turn down the University of Tokyo for that reason.

"Hath thy wits absconded?" Tsumugi asked, and when Ayame laughed spontaneously at her visible dismay, she inquired, "What, pray, brings thee such mirth?"

"Is my jest not obvious to thee? The University of Tokyo's halls were never mine own dreams. And after taking counsel, it seems the same university as thee would extend mine horizon beyond teaching."

Ayame's family was steeped in academia—her father was a university professor, her mother was a junior high school principal, and both her brothers were high-school teachers. Tsumugi knew well that Ayame aspired to work in dementia care for the elderly. Plus, the university Tsumugi planned on attending had a strong caregiving program.

"Don't scare me like that."

"Oh, I'm sorry, Tsumugi. I'm sorry."

"By the way..." Tsumugi suddenly said in a hushed tone, leaning closer to Ayame. "Is it true that sitting in one of the café's seats affords thee a ticket to go back in time?"

"He-he, 'tis absolutely true."

Ayame's reply was quick. Almost too quick—as if she had been anticipating the question.

"And this seat of such notoriety...which one is it?"

"That would be the one behind us."

Tsumugi looked over Ayame's shoulder to see a seat on which the woman in the white dress was sitting.

"What's this? It appears a fellow patron doth occupy that seat."

"Indeed, it does."

"Then what be the course of action?"

"Rumor holds that yon patron rises but once a day to seek the privy."

"Seek the privy?"

"Verily. The time to seize the seat is then."

"And upon seizing it?"

"A coffee is poured, and thou can visit the time of thy choosing."

"I see..."

"Tsumugi, if thou could journey the annals of time, when would thy destination be?"

"Me? If 'tis me thou ask, I wouldst surely choose the years between 1469 and 1487."

"Surely you jest?"

"No, 'tis indeed my wish to go there. Just one glimpse of Kumamoto Castle being erected from its stone walls—that hath ever been mine dream."

"Thy dream is grand indeed. Going back in time would be the only way to realize it. Trust thee, Tsumugi, to hold such a wish."

"Ayame, when would thy destination be?"

"Myself? Verily, I have yet to make up mine mind."

"Why not?"

"The many choices doth confound me. To single out but one is beyond me."

"Aye, then thou should bide a while before venturing through the halls of time, at least until thy mind is made up."

"Indeed, I should wait for a brief spell."

However, in this café, although you can travel to the

time you desire, you can't move from the seat you're sitting in or leave the café. There's also a time limit: you can only stay in the past until your cup of coffee has got cold, which is just a matter of minutes. So there was no way Tsumugi could see the castle being built, as she dreamed.

After that day, the two never visited the café together again.

Spring break rolled around, and Tsumugi came to hear some unsettling gossip.

"Apparently, Hayato Nanase confessed to Ayame but she turned him down."

Whether or not the rumor was true, it did not change how unsettled it made her feel, and the fact that Ayame had not mentioned it made it worse.

Why wouldn't she tell me?

Ayame had no reason to hide it from her. She could hardly know what that other boy had said to Tsumugi in junior high school. Only Tsumugi knew her pain from experiencing this a second time. So why was Ayame keeping quiet about Hayato's confession?

Was it because she knows I like Hayato and doesn't want to hurt my feelings?

Such are the ironies of life. Ever since hearing the rumor, Tsumugi felt an indescribable irritation nagging at her. On two occasions, the target of her affection had expressed his longing for Ayame. It was just a coincidence. Her rational mind understood that, but she had yet to accept it emotionally.

Why is it always Ayame?

If it was any other girl, she might have just accepted it. If Hayato had confessed to a stranger, she might have been able to cry in front of Ayame and forget about it.

But because it was Ayame, things were different.

Everyone I like ends up falling for Ayame.

Ayame is better than me.

What's wrong with me?

Is it because Ayame is cute? Am I simply not attractive?

These concerns continued to gnaw at her.

Ayame hasn't done anything wrong. It's not like she's intentionally trying to steal someone away from me. The person I like just happens to like Ayame and is choosing her over me. And yet I can't stop my negative feelings toward Ayame building up. Part of me wishes Ayame wasn't around. What if there's a third time?

Tsumugi was also struggling with two conflicting feelings: she wished Ayame had told her about the confession, but at the same time, she worried that doing so would have made things awkward.

Ayame was likely just as unsure about when and how to tell me.

No matter how she told me, it would only make me feel more inferior.

So it was that Tsumugi reached her conclusion.

I don't want to hear it. I don't want to know.

It was during spring break that Tsumugi had heard the rumor, and she made it a point to avoid Ayame thereafter. Unlike high school, their courses were in different departments of the university. This made it easier to continue steering clear of her even after classes commenced, and the days without meeting her began to grow.

Then, one day, the following transpired.

Tsumugi was walking around campus with a new male friend when she ran into Ayame by chance. Ayame spoke to Tsumugi in her usual archaic language.

"Ah, Tsumugi! 'Tis long since last we met, is it not? Art thou in good spirits?"

"Er, yeah."

"I, too, have now made up mine mind."

"About what?"

"On deciding on the past to which I wish to return at yon café. Dost thou not remember?"

"Oh, right. That conversation."

"Is something ailing thee?"

"Er, no, it's just that I might be late for my next class."

"Ah, I beg thy pardon. We have not met in ages. I got carried away in my joy to see thee."

"Er, yeah. Well then."

"Indeed."

With her male friend looking on, Tsumugi muddled through the conversation, offering only half-hearted and vague mumblings. She felt vaguely guilty doing this considering Ayame was simply acting as always, but the unconfirmed rumor that Hayato had confessed to Ayame still lingered in her mind.

I'll keep my distance for now. Once I've sorted out my feelings, we can be friends like before, Tsumugi told herself.

But then things took a turn for the worse.

Her new male friend whispered to her, "Is that girl a friend of yours, Tsumugi? She's cute, isn't she? Introduce me to her sometime, okay?"

"What?"

Something inside Tsumugi snapped. Not again. The root of her annoyance was jealousy. *As long as I'm with Ayame, I won't find happiness.*

From that day, Tsumugi began to avoid Ayame even more, and by the time they graduated from university, they had lost all contact with each other.

"This happened six years ago," Tsumugi said to conclude the story she was telling Kazu, the café waitress, who was busy behind the counter.

She was expecting an understanding remark, such as,

"Oh well, small misunderstandings can lead to friends drifting apart. These things happen." However, such words were not forthcoming. Kazu was reticent by nature and her reply was brief.

"Is that so?" she said, without any hint of emotion.

Kazu was responsible for pouring the coffee that allowed people to go back in time. She had a fair complexion and almond-shaped eyes, with a neat and unremarkable appearance: in short, nondescript.

Instead, a woman in a kimono sitting at the counter muttered, "Do you realize how shallow you sound?" Her name was Yaeko Hirai, but everyone called her Hirai.

She used to run a tiny bar in the neighborhood and was a café regular until three years ago. Now she ran a traditional inn in the Aoba ward of Sendai city in Miyagi Prefecture, which had been in business for more than a hundred and eighty years. Every year on this day she showed up at the café for a few hours. She had once gone back in time to meet her sister, who died in a traffic accident. That was on the 2nd of August, exactly three years ago.

"What?" It took Tsumugi aback to be called "shallow" by Hirai, still a stranger to her, who just happened to be in the café at the same time. She hadn't shared her story to be heard by Hirai, nor had she asked for her opinion—let alone to be criticized in such a way. It was far from the empathy she had been hoping for.

I don't think that's any of your business.

Tsumugi swallowed the words that had risen to her throat. She didn't have the courage to speak her feelings openly to a stranger.

Hirai continued, "No matter how you look at it, your friend Ayame must have really wanted to go to the same university as you. She must've turned down Tokyo University to be with you. How can you not understand that? I pity her, choosing you for her friend."

"Er, excuse me…"

Tsumugi, feeling overwhelmed by Hirai's flamboyant appearance, was looking to Kazu behind the counter for some help, but Kazu wouldn't even meet her gaze. Without the courage to speak her mind, Tsumugi was left looking bewildered.

Hirai abruptly swiveled on her stool to face Tsumugi directly and continued her barrage of truth bombs.

"The boy you liked confessed to your friend. And that petty reason was enough to get you all sulky. It's women like you I dislike the most," she stated bluntly.

"Hirai, that's quite enough," Kazu cut in, unable to ignore the situation any longer.

But Hirai was not finished with her sermon.

"Listen, love's a battlefield. Look at you. Too timid

to pass a simple Valentine's chocolate and captured by jealousy, a girl like you will never find happiness. If you love him, say it. If it doesn't work out, next! Men are everywhere. Just expand your horizons. No good man ever showed up for a woman who just waits around. It's a game of who confesses first. Men are also trying to figure out our feelings. Be forthright. And remember, it's a numbers game—the more you try, the better your chances. The more you hesitate, the more you lose. Get it?"

"O-okay," Tsumugi said, wounded by Hirai's words, which were outrageously blunt but at the same time refreshingly cutting. Still, for her, it felt like adding salt to an open wound. She bit her lip, her gaze dropping to the floor.

"Hirai, that's a bit harsh, don't you think?"

Unable to bear seeing Tsumugi like that, Kazu had uncharacteristically stepped in.

"Well, I just feel for that Ayame girl. I can't stand people who wreck their relationships out of petty jealousy. Are you happy being so self-centered?"

"I'm sorry," Tsumugi blurted out, her heart stinging from Hirai's poignant observations. Yet, oddly enough, her words had a liberating undertone to them.

Maybe, deep down, I had wanted someone to call me out.

As she pondered this, it felt like Hirai's words were chipping away at dark feelings festering deep inside her.

Hirai couldn't be stopped once she got going.

"That Hayato guy, if you had tried dating him, he could've been a narcissist who's all looks, am I right? You can't know a man until you try. Some tough-looking guys act like babies when you're alone with them, and the ones who seem to be the most serious about a relationship are often the most unfaithful. Hayato confessed to Ayame and got rejected, didn't he? Wasn't that your chance? Oh, but wait, that's old news now, isn't it? Okay, it might have been an opportunity back then, but no use sulking over it now. Rejected guys are easy to win over with a little kindness. Who cares who he likes? What matters is what you feel for him, how much you're into him, or am I off base here?"

"You're not."

Tsumugi felt Hirai had hit the nail on the head. Now, at twenty-eight, she understood. If she could redo it a different way, she'd jump at the chance. If only she had heard Hirai's words in the past.

But back then, I was young.

She was inexperienced in love and at an age when her emotions often got the better of her.

As a result, she was here now, once again revisiting this café carried by a wish to go back to that day.

Three days earlier, Tsumugi had attended her high-school reunion for the first time.

She had dodged several previous invitations since graduation, mostly because the thought of facing Ayame made her uneasy. She decided to attend this time partly because Hayato Nanase, the organizer, had personally reached out to her, and partly because she'd heard Ayame had only gone to the first reunion.

Even though it was called a reunion, many years had passed since high school, so the gathering wasn't large, just around ten people including Tsumugi and Hayato. Most were single, and the reunion felt more like a pretext for a boozy night out. With their thirties approaching, Tsumugi wondered if some were hoping to find a partner.

The topic inevitably turned to who they had liked back in high school. Naturally, Tsumugi couldn't be honest with the object of her affection right in front of her, so she mentioned the name of a random man who wasn't attending. "Seriously?" and 'No way!" The atmosphere was charged with surprise and amusement.

"Tsumugi, I thought you and Ayame were an item," one man said.

"Yeah, me too," chimed in another.

"Same here," said some of the others.

"What? Ayame and me?"

"Oh, come on. You two were always together, having weird conversations like 'what sayest thou?' and 'verily so,' remember?"

"No, that was just..."

Tsumugi sighed inwardly. What a childish perspective, typical of junior high or high schoolers.

"Not that I have any issue with it. I'm not prejudiced in that way. I mean, as long as it's two women. Two guys might bother me," said one man.

"Oh, it's the opposite for me. I don't mind if it's love between two boys. But such relationships between girls make me uncomfortable," said one of the women.

"That's the very definition of 'prejudice'—you two are aware of that, aren't you?"

Tsumugi had no memories of these classmates ever mingling with her, a castle geek, back in high school. Yet here they were now, making her relationship with Ayame the subject of gossip.

They probably just mentioned it to liven the conversation. Denying it would be a hassle. Tsumugi sighed inwardly again.

"That was a long time ago. I have a husband now," she said, raising her left ring finger.

"What? You're married? Why wasn't I invited to the wedding?"

"We never had a wedding ceremony."

"Why not?"

"I'm not good with such things."

Tsumugi always had a hard time with ceremonies, her high-school graduation included. With their marriage, they had filed the paperwork, but she regarded even that as a needless formality.

"Come on. Don't most women dream of a fancy wedding?"

"Do they?"

"I, for one, would want one."

"Have you met your Mr. Right?"

"Well, I'm still searching for him."

As the chatter carried on, Tsumugi felt strangely detached.

No one cares about my past with Ayame now. Though once classmates, we haven't been in touch for years. On graduation day, how many cried, saying they didn't want to part? They've probably forgotten they ever cried. Flushed it from their minds. Even my feelings for Hayato, someone I had a crush on, have vanished. Now I don't know why his confession to Ayame hurt me. Was I smitten with him that much? When I think about it, the past with Ayame is just ancient history. If Ayame were here, she'd laugh it off, saying, "I can't believe we did those things."

Ayame must have moved on. I'm merely an old friend she hasn't spoken to in a decade. It's all past. Probably just me fretting over it. I should forget it. It's not like I can change anything…

Tsumugi gulped her mug of beer. She decided to put things out of her mind for the night and enjoy the evening.

"By the way, we had the same conversation with Ayame at the first reunion," said someone.

"Same conversation? What do you mean?"

"About you and Ayame being an item."

"What?"

"Oh, come on. Let's drop it," interjected Hayato.

"What's wrong with talking about it? You were there, remember? Like tonight, everyone was chiming in, agreeing…and then Ayame suddenly burst into tears…"

What?

"Okay, end of discussion!"

Hayato clapped his hands to change the subject.

"Let's move on to the after-party!"

"After-party? Let's do it! Where are we going?"

The guy who brought up Ayame seemed quite drunk. His name didn't ring a bell. Tsumugi was still struggling to place him in her memories. Yet his words had unsettled her. He, on the other hand, was now focused on the after-party.

"So…" Tsumugi began to ask why Ayame had cried but was stopped by Hayato.

"I'll tell you later."

After moving to the second party venue and waiting for the mood to liven up, Tsumugi called Hayato outside the bar to continue their conversation. It was now past nine in the evening. Hayato gave a bit of a preamble about how he usually hung out with the current crowd before turning to the subject of Ayame.

"Just a quick check..." he began.

"Yeah?"

"How much do you actually know about Ayame?"

"What are you getting at?"

Visibly perplexed, Tsumugi watched Hayato glance around suspiciously for a long time, as if ensuring Ayame wasn't eavesdropping.

"Actually, I confessed to Ayame. Right after high school, during spring break."

"Is that so?"

As Tsumugi answered, she was genuinely surprised at her own reaction. Her current calmness felt surreal compared to the turmoil she experienced at the time just by hearing the rumor. It was no slight to Hayato, but even hearing his confession directly now left her entirely unfazed.

Rather, her feelings were now focused on Ayame. "And then?"

"Well, actually, ever since we were in the same class in the first year of high school, I've liked Ayame."

"Oh, I didn't know."

Tsumugi tried to feign surprise, but it wasn't convincing.

I don't care about that now. Though, if I heard this back then, it might have upset me.

"The reason I studied so hard was to go to the same university as Ayame. I barely got into U-Tokyo, and then she turned it down, did you know?"

"Yes..."

Memories from those days flooded back. Ayame had everything Tsumugi desired. She was beautiful, clever, and effortlessly good at everything. And also, back then, Ayame was liked by the very person Tsumugi had feelings for. Repressed feelings of jealousy once more began seeping into her heart.

"I was shocked. Who in their right mind would turn down U-Tokyo? I was planning on confessing after we got to university and became closer friends."

Hayato gave a resigned shrug, suggesting he'd moved past the old disappointment, enough to even laugh about it.

"So, I panicked, told her how I felt, and she rejected me..."

Just then, Hayato's phone rang. He checked the screen and said, "Ah, sorry, mind if I take this?"

"Go ahead."

"What? What's up? I told you I was going to a reunion tonight, didn't I?"

From Hayato's tone, the caller seemed to be his girlfriend.

Tsumugi felt irritated. She couldn't see at all how Hayato getting rejected was connected to Ayame crying at the reunion.

Yet there was one thing she clearly realized.

What's this weird feeling of satisfaction I got on hearing Ayame was crying?

She had heard people say "the misery of others is as sweet as honey" and this felt exactly like that. She was attempting to derive a sense of happiness from hearing about Ayame's misery. That was what was bothering her.

Why had she cried?

I wish he'd get to the point. Why did Ayame cry?

She realized her impatience with Hayato was evidence that jealousy and envy, the dark emotions she had suppressed in the depths of her heart, were yearning for Ayame's misfortune.

I can't stand this.

She had avoided facing these emotions. By comparing herself with Ayame, she ended up cursing the unfairness of it all. It was this ugly part of herself she didn't want to acknowledge. Thus distancing herself from Ayame was her only solution.

But it had not solved anything.

I have just been suppressing my true feelings.

The embers of her jealousy still smoldered.

Yet, in that moment, she remembered.

I had genuinely wanted to be Ayame's friend. Without being stained by jealousy, I wanted to laugh with her and be close friends forever. Someone I could share everything with—including what pained and upset me. I had thought we could keep that kind of relationship, at least through high school.

But it didn't last. She hadn't spoken to Ayame in years and didn't even know where she was now.

She sighed heavily.

I can't bear feeling this miserable. I might gain some petty satisfaction from knowing why Ayame cried, but in return, I would lose part of my humanity. Being someone who revels in other people's misfortune because of my envy, I am bound to feel a sense of guilt when wishing for my future children to be kind.

Suddenly, she felt drained. Her irritation with Hayato evaporated.

She looked skyward.

"That's it for me tonight. I'm going home," she inadvertently said out loud.

As she pulled out her purse from her bag to pay her

share of the after-party she had barely attended, Hayato returned from his phone call.

"Sorry, sorry, where did we leave off?"

"Never mind, let's forget it. I'm going home now..."

"Oh, right. I got to the part where Ayame rejected me, didn't I?"

As if Tsumugi's words hadn't reached him, Hayato continued the conversation.

He hasn't changed at all. He never listened back then, either.

Tsumugi sighed softly.

"She told me after I confessed that she loved someone else."

"What?"

Tsumugi couldn't believe her ears.

Since we were classmates in junior high school, I never heard of Ayame liking anyone.

Tsumugi had times when she was interested in other boys, including seniors and juniors from her club activities—but even then, Ayame just listened to Tsumugi's stories with a smile.

Ayame had someone she liked?

Despite it being a matter from nearly a decade ago, Tsumugi couldn't hide her astonishment.

"Who was it?"

She asked the question without even realizing it. Still

clutching a banknote she'd pulled from her purse, her hand remained frozen in midair as she waited for Hayato's reply.

"Look, take this with a grain of salt because it's just my own hunch, but..."

Scratching his head and averting his gaze, Hayato stumbled over his words.

"What?"

"Could it be that Ayame liked you?"

"Excuse me?"

Just moments ago, Hayato had halted a conversation about Ayame and Tsumugi. Now he was circling back to it, and Tsumugi felt her head spinning.

"Don't joke."

"I'm not. Think about it—she was super-popular but turned down every boy who came her way. What else could explain it?"

"Huh?"

From Hayato's serious gaze, Tsumugi realized that this topic had a different intent from the previous "I thought you two were dating" conversation.

"Ayame liked me?"

As far as Tsumugi was concerned, they weren't actually dating, so it was not a topic she had to particularly deny. And it would be the same for Ayame.

However, if Ayame, a woman, had had feelings for Tsumugi, another woman, the story would change. Especially if Ayame didn't want anyone else to know about it, it wouldn't be surprising if she felt shocked when people speculated about her relationship with Tsumugi.

"That can't be true."

"But at the reunion, she cried and told me not to tell you. So maybe she didn't want you to know that she felt that way?"

Hayato avoided saying it outright, but Tsumugi got his drift.

Ayame had a romantic same-sex attraction to Tsumugi.

The world swayed before her eyes.

"No way..."

Tsumugi had seen Ayame as a friend. Considering their shared love for history, she even thought of her as a nerdy soulmate and someone she'd want to call her best friend if her jealousy had allowed it. But that was all.

While silence enveloped Tsumugi, Hayato let out a small sigh.

"But, well, there's no way to ever know how she felt now," he mumbled as if speaking to himself.

"What do you mean there's no way to ever know?"

"What?"

"You mean you don't know her address?"

In response, Hayato looked visibly uncomfortable.

"You don't know?"

I've got a bad feeling about this. I don't think I want to hear it.

"...Know what?"

However, she had no choice but to hear it. Her heart rate increased.

"I don't know the details, but I think it was cancer."

"Cancer?"

"I think it was the year after the reunion, so maybe seven or eight years ago now?"

I remember.

"Tell me you're lying."

"Sorry, I had no idea you were in the dark about it. Actually, I also found out later. No one I know was invited to the funeral. I just assumed you would've been..."

"It's so shocking..."

"Are you all right?"

Tsumugi covered her face with her hands and groaned. Then she looked up at the sky.

That was around the time I received a message from Ayame.

I have something important to talk about. I'll be waiting at that mysterious café we know about.

What Ayame wanted to convey at that time remained unknown. But Tsumugi had misconstrued the message's intent.

She finally feels like talking about the confession from Hayato?

That's what she had thought.

Too little, too late.

And with that frame of mind, she ignored the message.

How wrong she had been.

That evening, Tsumugi practically ran away from Hayato and the after-party.

"I couldn't have known Ayame's real situation, but that doesn't excuse me from ignoring Ayame's message without considering her feelings. If she's waiting for me, I want to go back to the past to meet her. Please, take me back to that day, the day she was waiting for me in this café," said Tsumugi with a deep bow.

"Mmm, mmm, I see, I see." Hirai, who had been listening at the counter seat, stood up and walked over to Tsumugi.

"You'd better go to her soon, then."

"Huh?"

"I mean, that's an important reason. You should've mentioned it sooner. What on earth has been holding you back? She did message you that she's waiting, didn't she?"

"Y-yes."

"Then you should go. The sooner the better."

Up until now, Hirai had been scolding Tsumugi, but

now she seemed ready to help, effectively commandeering the situation.

Tsumugi was also eager to travel back in time to reunite with Ayame, but there was a snag.

"To go back to the past, I have to wait for that woman to use the toilet, correct?"

Tsumugi looked over at the woman in the white dress, sitting in the café's furthest corner.

"My, you're well-informed."

"It's just what I heard when I came here back in high school."

Tsumugi shifted her gaze to a framed photo of Kei Tokita on the cash register. Her memory of Kei speaking in samurai language flashed through her mind.

"I see, I see." Hirai was not flustered. She knew the rules as well as anyone.

Over the counter, she signaled to Kazu. "Kazu, ah, could you…do the thing?" she asked, making a pouring gesture.

Tsumugi had no idea what Hirai was intending, but Kazu quietly disappeared into the kitchen.

"What exactly are you doing?"

"Actually, there's a way to make her get up against her will."

"How?"

Hirai, emanating a Jimmy Choo fragrance, locked her eyes on the woman in white and smiled cunningly.

"Don't worry. You'll be back in the past before you know it."

After a while, Kazu emerged from the kitchen, holding a carafe filled with coffee.

She stood next to the woman in the white dress and asked, "Would you care for some more coffee?"

Confused, Tsumugi gave Hirai a questioning look. Hirai, in turn, shook her head as if to say, *Just watch.*

"Yes, please."

The woman in the white dress carefully closed the book she was reading and drank the entire cup of coffee in front of her in one go. Kazu refilled the empty cup. Tsumugi couldn't make sense of this exchange.

"Would you care for another cup of coffee?"

"What?" Tsumugi couldn't help but exclaim.

The woman in the white dress hadn't even taken a sip of her refilled coffee yet.

"Um, ah…"

Tsumugi instinctively tried to interject, but Hirai stopped her.

"Shush. It's fine."

"But, but…"

While Tsumugi was still suspicious, they heard the woman's voice one more time.

"Yes, please."

"Eh?"

The woman in the white dress had, just like before, downed her cup of coffee in one go.

How strange…

Before Tsumugi had time to be shocked, Kazu immediately refilled the empty cup and asked again, "Would you care for another cup of coffee?"

While Tsumugi looked on, stunned, the third round ended as before.

"What's going on?"

"She can't say no when Kazu offers her coffee."

"Why is that?"

"It's a rule."

"Rule?"

"Yes. You've heard the other ones, haven't you? Like there is nothing that you can do in the past that will change the present, or that the only people you can meet while in the past are those who have visited the café—you know, a rule."

"You can't be serious?"

Hirai's gaze was on the two, caught in their endless loop of coffee refills.

"Look and see."

The moment Hirai muttered this, the woman in the

white dress downed her fifth cup of coffee and abruptly stood up.

"...oilet," she muttered.

"What did she say?"

Her voice was too soft to catch, making Tsumugi frown. But the destination was immediately clear. Weaving through the space between Tsumugi and Hirai, the woman in the white dress darted off to the toilet.

"There, the seat's free now."

Hirai, tugging at Tsumugi's puzzled hand, pushed her into the seat that would let her travel back to the past.

"You're aware of the rules, aren't you?"

"Er, ah, yeah."

"Great."

"But what should I say to her?"

"Well, she's waiting for you, isn't she?"

"What?"

"She has been waiting, all this while."

Hirai's large eyes, lashes flicking upward, looked straight into Tsumugi's. Lying in their depths was more than just seriousness; there was a weight, or perhaps a deep sadness.

"Then go to her."

"Why are you suddenly...?"

Tsumugi wanted to know why Hirai, a stranger, had become so cooperative.

"My sister was waiting, too. Waiting for me, forever."

"Oh?"

"And then she died. In a car accident."

"How tragic."

Tsumugi now understood the sadness she had sensed in the depths of Hirai's eyes.

"I still regret it. Why wasn't I kinder to my sister? Why didn't I listen to her properly? I was such a terrible sister."

Tears clouded Hirai's eyes as her voice wavered, but she spoke her truth. Maybe she saw her own regrets reflected in Tsumugi's.

"I couldn't save my sister even when I went to see her. I knew saying sorry wouldn't bring her back to life. But I still went. I wanted to see her face one more time. Despite all the awful things I did to her, I still loved her."

Tsumugi bit her lips as she absorbed Hirai's words.

"Even though you were jealous, you did care about her deeply, didn't you?"

"Yes, I did."

"You surely regret those actions now, don't you?"

"Yes."

"Then go to her. Reality won't change, no matter what you say. Just spill out everything you're feeling."

With tears in her eyes, Hirai flashed a cheeky grin.

"Okay, I will."

Tsumugi straightened her back and settled into the

chair that could take her into the past. She exhaled deeply.

Hirai resumed her seat at the counter when Kazu returned from the kitchen. On her tray were a silver kettle and a pristine white coffee cup.

"Shall we proceed?"

Kazu stood beside Tsumugi and placed the empty white coffee cup in front of her, her thin almond-shaped eyes directed on Tsumugi.

"I will now pour the coffee."

It was only at this moment that Tsumugi noticed the slightly chilly air surrounding her. She also felt a greater presence emanating from Kazu, who had been unimposing until now, and the atmosphere in the café was suddenly taut and solemn.

Kazu continued her explanation.

"The only time you will have when you go back to the past is from the moment the cup is filled with coffee until it gets completely cold. Is that clear?"

"Yes."

Tsumugi answered without fully understanding, but by her estimation, the coffee would take about ten to fifteen minutes to cool. It was a short window, but that was the rule, and there was no point in arguing.

I don't expect to be forgiven.

Though this thought made Tsumugi uneasy, there was one thing she had no doubts about.

But if I don't go, I feel like I'll regret it forever.

Tsumugi met Kazu's gaze and announced her decision.

"Let's do it."

Kazu nodded slightly, seeming to understand Tsumugi's resolve.

She improved her posture and placed her hand on the silver kettle. "Then before the coffee gets cold," she whispered.

Silently, the cup was filled with coffee. The rising ebony surface clearly reflected the ceiling fan.

Beautiful.

Tsumugi's eyes were glued on the filling cup.

Eventually, the cup was full, and a wisp of steam began to rise. Then an inexplicable sensation enveloped Tsumugi; neither sleepiness nor dizziness could aptly describe it.

How could I be getting sleepy at a time like this?

Her instinct to rub her eyes led to a shocking discovery.

"Eh?"

What she had thought was her hand had blended with the steam rising from the coffee. Before she realized it, the surrounding scenery began to distort.

Am I…floating?

Too surprised to fully grasp the situation, she shouted, "Wait! Wait!"

She didn't even know to whom she was saying "wait." Her mind was in complete panic. Soon, ever-changing scenes cascaded down around her at incredible speed. Caught in an unexpected turn of events, she screamed as if she were on a roller coaster.

"Help me—!"

As her consciousness began to fade, montage sequences of memories of days spent with Ayame flashed through her mind.

"Art thou ensnared by love's sweet grasp?"

"Nay!" denied Tsumugi.

"The object of thy affection is Hayato, is it not?"

"N-n-nay, how dost thou…?"

"One can tell just by looking."

"Nay."

"I have thee well and truly seen through."

"I am undone."

"Since 'tis so, why not proffer some sweets on next month's Valentine's Day?"

"Sweets, thou sayest?"

"Verily, the day of our parting—our graduation—is

nigh. Valentine's Day is thy last good chance. Canst thee afford to let it slip by?"

"Indeed." Tsumugi was warming to the idea.

"We part ways in university, what's there to fret about?"

"Indeed, indeed."

"Brace thyself and step forth."

How ironic, looking back, that it was Ayame saying this with a smile. I was oblivious of Ayame's feelings toward me.

If only I was as cute as her.

I envied her.

That was simply how it was. I would hear a rumor.

"Did you hear? Asakura from Class 3 mustered the courage to confess to her?"

The fact that overhearing such rumors was unsettling was undeniable.

Will Hayato be one of them?

The anxiety continually resurfaces.

"But it seems Asakura got rejected."

"Again?"

Ayame doesn't seem interested in having a boyfriend.

Why? Because she has high standards?

Hayato is looking at Ayame.

Has he eyes for her, too?

Why is it that all the boys I like are constantly looking at Ayame?

I'm not Ayame.

I'm not as cute as she is.

My envy is turning into jealousy.

I hate her, even though she's my friend.

I feel my heart steadily darken.

"Hayato Nanase apparently confessed to Ayame, but she turned him down."

How could I continue liking Hayato after he got rejected, with the knowledge that he liked Ayame at the back of my mind?

"I'm sorry, Tsumugi, but I actually like Ayame," those words, told to me back in junior high school. Those words never left my mind. They have never left. The same cycle repeats. As long as I'm with Ayame, I will have to confront my darkest emotions.

If only Ayame weren't there.

Ayame did nothing wrong.

Even so...

Upon becoming university students, Ayame continued to talk in samurai language, so I ended up telling her, "Look, we're not in high school anymore. Could you stop that?"

I distanced myself from her. It was all me.

I knew it at the time...that it was my jealousy.

That's why I ended up ignoring Ayame's last message.

Now I want to see her and talk in person.

Ayame is waiting.

At that mysterious café, forever...

As if waking from sleep, Tsumugi slowly opened her eyes.

It was the same familiar café interior which met her gaze. Shaded lamps hung from the ceiling, three large antique pendulum clocks were fixed to the wall, and a wooden ceiling fan rotated slowly overhead.

However, Kazu, who had poured her coffee, was nowhere to be found. Instead, standing behind the counter was Kei Tokita, staring back at Tsumugi with big round eyes. She was wearing a light beige cardigan and a wine-red apron with a chest bib.

"Ah."

"Hello. Welcome!"

Kei's greeting was noticeably different from Kazu's emotionless monotone. She, always expressive, lit up with an unreserved, genuine smile as she welcomed the newly arrived Tsumugi. Her eyes sparkled as if to say, *I've been waiting for you!*

"Ah, um."

Kei pointed her index finger upward.

"She's outside on the phone right now. You see, the signal doesn't reach down here."

Tsumugi had experienced no signal a few times, too, when she frequented this basement café.

"I see."

Tsumugi was perplexed by Kei's response. It was as if Kei knew she would be coming from the future.

"Shall I call her for you?"

"No, I'm fine."

Tsumugi immediately regretted her rushed answer. If she was living in the past, she could wait for Ayame to come back leisurely. But now was different. There was a time limit. She had to finish her coffee before it got cold. She touched the cup; it was still sufficiently warm, though not hot. She could gulp it down if she tried. Certainly less hot than she had anticipated.

What should I do? Maybe I should ask her to fetch Ayame after all…

"Hast ye been embroiled in a quarrel, perchance?" Kei asked while Tsumugi was feeling the cup's warmth in her palm, and deliberating.

"What?"

Tsumugi's head snapped up. She was taken aback by Kei's uncanny perception of her dispute with Ayame. But hearing Kei speak in the samurai tongue was like a stab to the chest. Tsumugi felt the pain of memories piercing her heart—memories of happily chatting in this café. She remembered saying, "Look, we're not in high school anymore. Could you stop that?" After she had pushed Ayame away, she had been rejecting that samurai speech ever since.

What if Ayame doesn't come back?

Suddenly anxious, Tsumugi decided to take back what she had said.

"Um, perhaps—"

As soon as their eyes met, Kei replied, "I shall summon her forthwith!" and sprinted toward the exit.

"Um, perhaps..."

CLANG-DONG

It all happened in a blink of an eye.

"Sorry, you must be feeling rushed." Nagare Tokita, the café's owner, emerged from the kitchen, wearing a cook's uniform. Nagare was a towering man, nearly two meters tall. He narrowed his thin eyes with an apologetic expression, seemingly regretful of Kei's meddling. "My wife is thinking about the time constraint and wants to give her the chance to meet you as soon as possible."

Tsumugi felt a snag in his words, "to give her the chance to meet you."

Not for me to meet her?

It was a subtle nuance, but if what Nagare said was true, it suggested that Kei harbored a considerable amount of sympathy toward Ayame. Noticing Tsumugi's reaction, Nagare quickly elaborated.

"She waited for you here for five hours…"

"What?"

"Given her persistent nature, my wife tried her best to engage her in conversation. However, despite her efforts, she was unable to even get a smile out of her."

Tsumugi winced upon hearing Nagare's explanation, and her chest tightened.

I made Ayame wait for five hours.

Nagare continued. "Then you appeared from the future. People who decide to return to the past despite learning about the complicated rules and risks must have a compelling reason. You likely missed this day at the café and are now regretful. Am I right?"

Taking a deep breath, Tsumugi could only muster, "…Yes."

She looked at the three pendulum clocks. She had heard during her high-school days that only the one in the middle worked accurately. Now it pointed to four in the afternoon.

Ayame must have stayed until closing time.

Just imagining it angered her at the discourtesy she had committed. Now she felt regret for driving Ayame to this point over something so trivial.

But as if reading her thoughts, Nagare muttered quietly, "As with anyone else who has chosen to sit in that seat, I'm sure there is a great deal on your mind."

Tsumugi thought that Nagare had likely seen his fair share of regretful souls in this café.

It's not just me.

This tiny revelation lent some buoyancy to her sinking spirits.

"Will it be a long conversation?"

"Pardon?"

"Your conversation with her."

Nagare wasn't prying into what they'd be discussing, but rather how long it would take. There was only one reason for this: she only had until the coffee went completely cold.

What will happen?

Even the pettiest of reasons can delay the mending of a relationship. Often neither side accepts the claims of the other and it can remain strained for many years. Human hearts are complicated, and simple solutions often elude them. The more you believe in someone, the more unbearable the anger or sorrow becomes when you feel betrayed. Would it end with a one-sided apology, or perhaps only complicate matters more? Perhaps it might end with Ayame unleashing her dissatisfaction. Tsumugi had no way of telling.

But...

Tsumugi didn't think that a complicated relationship could be restored within the brief time it takes for a cup of coffee to go cold. Therefore, she honestly replied, "I can't say for sure."

"I see," Nagare responded, as if he had expected her answer. "In that case, let me put this in your coffee."

He stood beside Tsumugi holding something that looked like a toothpick. However, upon closer inspection, it just looked so in Nagare's large hand. It was actually a silvery metallic rod.

"What's that for?"

"It goes in your cup. It will start beeping just before the coffee goes completely cold. When it does, please be sure to finish your coffee immediately, even if you're in the middle of talking."

"It's an alarm?"

"Yes."

Nagare held the metal rod in front of Tsumugi and then placed it into the full cup of coffee. It was about the size of a small spoon.

"You're aware of what occurs if your coffee gets cold before you finish it, aren't you?"

Tsumugi had heard this while visiting the café with Ayame back in high school.

Something about becoming a ghost and having to sit in this chair forever.

At the time, she had dismissed it as ludicrous. But after actually traveling back in time, she was beginning to wonder if it might be true.

A ghost?

A chill ran down her spine.

"Are you all right?"

Tsumugi looked up to see concern on Nagare's face.

"I'm fine," she replied.

CLANG-DONG

Drawn by the sound of the bell, Tsumugi glanced toward the entrance.

Out of sight beyond the arch-shaped entrance was the café's large wooden door, upon which was attached a bell like a cowbell. So at this point, Ayame was still out of sight. Despite that, Tsumugi's shoulders tensed and her heart was pounding as she clenched her fists on her knees.

"Look, we're not in high school anymore. Could you stop that?"

That single line, which Tsumugi had shot at Ayame because she was still using samurai language at university, nagged at her, causing Ayame's sorrowful reaction to resurface in her mind.

"Come on in," a voice called out from beyond the archway.

She's just around the corner.

A rush of adrenaline coursed through her.

It was during her second year of university that Tsumugi received the message that Ayame would be waiting in this café. This would make the Ayame on the other side of the arch twenty years old. Tsumugi, for her part, was now twenty-eight. Now a whole eight years separated them; Ayame was not only the fairer but now the younger, providing clear reason for Tsumugi to have reservations about seeing her. During their high-school days, when they were in the same swimming club, Ayame had maintained her exceptionally fair skin, even in summer. Her distinct features, which had no need for makeup, had already made her stand out among the female students in the school.

No doubt she would be only more beautiful.

An honest assessment of Tsumugi's feelings at that moment would be a tug-of-war between wanting and not wanting to see Ayame.

Life is so unfair.

Tsumugi had muttered this in front of the mirror so many times—in high school, university, her first job, her first date with a workmate, and even after they broke up. Every time she looked in the mirror, certain emotions surged as her round face, marked with freckles and sunspots and a small nose, stared back at her with puffy eyes.

If only I could be as cute as Ayame.

But now that she had heard how Ayame felt, new questions began to surface.

What did Ayame find good about me?

Tastes vary, of course. There's not always a rhyme or reason to who you fall for. Looking back, Tsumugi didn't even know why she had fallen for Hayato. But why did Ayame choose her?

Because we were both castle geeks?

But then, wouldn't any castle enthusiast do?

Other thoughts also wormed their way in.

If I were a guy, I would have totally fallen for Ayame. Being a castle geek and that beautiful, it would be weird not to fall for her. But I would surely get turned down. Because Ayame doesn't like men; she likes me, a woman…

Just then,

"It hath been a long while, hath it not?"

It was Ayame.

Bringing with her that peculiar samurai speech with exaggerated intonation, she sounded exactly as she had in high school. Her voice, such a luscious, calm alto.

"Look, we're not in high school anymore. Could you stop that?"

Ever since that day, she no longer got to hear Ayame's samurai speech. Upon hearing it again, Tsumugi's heart was instantly pulled back to high school. But only for a fleeting moment.

"...Huh?"

She was snapped back to reality when she saw Ayame standing before the entrance.

"Ayame?"

"What is that look thou dost display?"

The woman tapped her head as she sat down in the seat across from Tsumugi.

I shouldn't stare.

Even so, Tsumugi's gaze couldn't stray from Ayame's head. She couldn't look away.

Her skin once as fair and translucent as porcelain was now ghastly pale. She still had her large eyes, but other than that, there was nothing reminiscent of Tsumugi's high-school bestie Ayame. Her luscious black hair, once akin to silk, had all fallen out. But it was more than her hair; her arms, exposed at the ends of her sweater sleeves, were thin and frail. Even through her clothes it was evident that her muscular swimmer's physique had dramatically withered away.

This can't be real.

Tsumugi's mind went blank.

"Egad! Camest thou unknowing of mine condition?"

Ayame said this with a gentle smile, but loneliness filled her expression. In other words, she read from Tsumugi's face that in the years ahead Tsumugi would not get in touch with her.

I can't bear to look.

Even though she had heard about Ayame's passing, Tsumugi hadn't expected to see her changed to this extent. She felt the urge to gulp down her coffee and flee.

"How many years dost thee claim?"

"What?"

"Thine age."

"T-twenty-eight."

"What? Twenty-eight? Thou hast not changed a whit."

That was hardly true. An eight-year difference cannot be hidden. Tsumugi had undoubtedly aged. But how could she respond to a comment about appearances after seeing Ayame so transformed?

"Hmm? What's this!"

Ayame's eyes caught sight of Tsumugi's hand.

"Art thou wed?"

"Huh? Ah..."

In a split second, Tsumugi hid her left ring finger.

Could it be that Ayame liked you?

Remembering the words she'd heard from Hayato, Tsumugi was concerned that Ayame would be hurt seeing the ring.

I messed up.

Tsumugi averted her gaze from Ayame, hid her left hand under the table, and unwittingly lifted her coffee cup with her right. Ayame watched her and quietly sighed.

"What dost thou find unsettling? Pray don't tell me thy companion is Hayato?"

"What? Unthinkable!"

Before she knew it, she had replied in a similar samurai style of speech. A spur-of-the-moment impulse, perhaps to distract from her error of exposing her ring.

Ayame erupted into laughter upon hearing Tsumugi's vehement denial. Tsumugi also laughed, not knowing why she had refused so assertively.

"I forever wonder what charm thou didst find in Hayato back then."

"I was but youthful. I, too, wondered that upon our meeting at a reunion."

Both of them broke into laughter again.

"What sort of man is thine husband?"

"Naught but a geek."

"Is that so?"

"He hath more knowledge of history than even I."

"A remarkable feat if true."

"Aye. Once he commences speaking of great warriors, he doth not stop."

"Which of the great warriors doth he favor?"

"The gigantic Magara Naotaka."

"The towering warrior who wielded the eight-foot sword?"

"None other."

"Verily, a geek he must be."

"Indeed."

Again, they both laughed. Tsumugi was surprised how easily her speech changed to the language of the samurai; it somehow felt fitting. She decided to continue in the same vein.

However, something vital had slipped her mind.

Beep, beep, beep… Beep, beep, beep…

The alarm indicating the coffee was soon to get cold was resounding throughout the café.

"Ah!" The smile fell from Tsumugi's face.

But we haven't had any time to chat. I need a little longer.

She cast a pleading gaze at Kei and Nagare behind the counter. Kei averted her eyes while Nagare slowly shook his head apologetically.

"It's not fair…"

Tsumugi was on the verge of tears.

Yet…

What?

Ayame, sitting opposite her, was smiling. They had learned of the café's rule during high school, but she was unaware of the alarm that Nagare had given Tsumugi.

"Alas, Ayame…"

"I know. The time has come."

"I…I…"

Tsumugi felt she must apologize, but the more she tried to, the more elusive such words became. A nagging question popped into her mind: What good would an apology do?

Beep, beep, beep, beep…

But time waits for no one. From the counter, Kei's concerned eyes told Tsumugi that she was running out of time. She even imagined Kei might forcibly pour it down her throat.

Better drink it now.

Tsumugi grabbed the cup, but still…

I can't just leave like this!

…she couldn't bring herself to lift the cup to her lips.

"Drink swiftly," Ayame whispered softly.

"Why art thou so calm?"

"If thou wert to become a ghost here, how could I sleep at night? Precious little of mine life remains, so please spare me from additional torment," said Ayame with a hearty chuckle.

Stop it! Now I have no choice but to drink!

"Sorry, Tsumugi."

It was as if Ayame saw right through Tsumugi's feelings. She had said that on purpose.

"This is not fair!"

Closing her eyes, Tsumugi gulped down the coffee.

"So we say farewell," Ayame announced, pulling a ribbon-tied box from her shoulder bag and placing it in front of Tsumugi.

"What's this?"

Fighting the floating sensation enveloping her, Tsumugi took the box.

"'Tis chocolate."

"Chocolate?"

"It is Valentine's, after all."

This fact had escaped Tsumugi, who had come from the future. She had forgotten until now that their meeting was scheduled for the 14th of February.

"For me?"

"To express my feelings."

"Oh…"

Judging by Ayame's flushed ears, it was clearly not the "chocolate between friends" that is exchanged among girls nowadays.

"Indeed," said Ayame.

"But…but…"

"I understand. 'Tis not that I desire anything particular… I merely wished to express myself."

"At such timing, though…"

"It would be fair to call me cunning, but I've awaited

this moment. I have no time left to mend my relationship with thee, is that not so?"

There were no words to counter Ayame's pointed remark.

"But here, in this café, I could wait an eternity. I believed that even after my passing, a future thee might one day come to see me."

"Why...why didn't you say something sooner...?"

"I knew full well that thou wouldst not be ready to accept what I spoke."

"But..."

"Who couldst not even bestow chocolates on Hayato?"

"That's different."

"It is one and the same."

"How?"

"The agony of not winning thy gaze is the same," Ayame said, distorting her face as she tried to smile. Then she added with a more melancholic murmur, "But to die without ever conveying my feelings is an even greater torment." Her softer tone was perhaps intended to spare Tsumugi—who couldn't reciprocate her feelings—the pain, but it reached Tsumugi's ears, nonetheless.

"Ah..."

Tsumugi felt adrift in space as her body's transmutation into misty vapor began.

"W-wait!"

She reached out toward Ayame, but even her hand had lost its shape. Now fully in vaporous form, she began getting sucked up into the ceiling.

"Ayame!"

"Farewell."

"Ayame!"

"Rest easy, I will not be expecting anything in return on White Day!"

Those were Ayame's last words, half in jest and half sincere. Though she smiled broadly as she watched Tsumugi ascend into the ceiling, large tears streamed from her eyes.

"Ayame! Aya…" Tsumugi completely disappeared, only her voice faintly resonating. "…me…"

Before anyone knew it, the woman in the white dress sat where Tsumugi had been.

"She's gone."

Staring at the ceiling through which Tsumugi had disappeared, Ayame covered her face with both hands, her shoulders shaking violently.

"Tsumugi…"

It was Kei who supported Ayame, now on the verge of collapsing.

"You did well."

Ayame cried out loud in Kei's arms.

"So, Tsumugi awaits on the other side of this door, is that right?"

Standing in front of the large door of the basement café, Ayame posed this question to Kei behind her. Ayame was wearing a wig to conceal her balding scalp.

"Yes..." Kei said. Then, seeing Ayame breathing heavily after having run down the stairs in her weakened condition, she asked, "...but are you okay?"

"I'm okay."

Ayame put her hand on her chest, steadying her breathing.

"I fell for her the moment I laid eyes on her," she confessed shyly, more to herself than to anyone else.

She continued, "The day I transferred schools, Tsumugi was sitting all the way at the back. She was everything I'd ever wanted—absolutely adorable."

Her hand now grasped the doorknob, hesitantly but determinedly.

"From that day on, she was all I could see. I even faked being into her castle obsession to get her attention. The first time I spoke to her, I thought my heart would explode. It was my happiest moment. But when Hayato confessed to me, I had a sinking feeling. I had already caused her the same heartache back in junior high."

Though Tsumugi had never told Ayame why the boy in junior high school had turned her down, Ayame knew anyway.

"I actually regret that I never confessed to her what I felt. If only I had shared my feelings on Valentine's Day back when I fell in love with her. Oh, I know she probably would have rejected me, but at least it would have stopped her suffering later. I realize that now. My presence alone caused her distress. So I'm here to say sorry for the hurt I caused."

Her hand tightened on the doorknob, but before she could turn it, Kei interjected.

"You've got it wrong," she said, her words tinged with an unmistakable tone of disapproval.

"Got it wrong? How?"

Ayame turned around with widened eyes, surprised by Kei's unexpected words.

"If you had confessed then, wouldn't it have been just a schoolgirl crush? And precisely because you didn't, you were able to make real memories with her, correct?"

"Real memories?"

"Yes. Had you confessed, you might have avoided causing her some distress, but neither you nor Tsumugi would have ended up with anything to remember."

"Tsumugi neither?"

"She would prefer to have the memories with you. Of course she would. Otherwise, why would she go to such lengths to meet you like this?"

"I see..."

"In life, you bundle up the good and the bad—they're all memories."

Tears brimmed and fell from Ayame's eyes at Kei's words.

"No time for tears. She's waiting."

"Right."

Wiping her tear-streaked face, Ayame removed her now slightly dislodged wig.

"Thank you. I was close to making a last-minute regret. I'll show her my true self, and this gift that I never got to give her..."

From her shoulder bag, Ayame pulled out a small box. It was wrapped in crimson paper with a gold ribbon. It also had a message card tucked in.

"I'd like her to have it," Ayame said, then swung open the large café door and stepped inside.

Slowly, as if emerging from a dream, Tsumugi floated back to reality. Ayame was no longer in front of her. She scanned the café. Kei, who had been anxiously watching them from behind the counter, was gone, and in her place was Kazu. Unlike Kei, who looked like she might burst into tears at any moment, Kazu's face betrayed no emotion. She merely watched the unfolding events with cool detachment.

Could it all have been a dream?

Tsumugi tried believing it was, but the ribboned box that remained in her hands wouldn't allow it. Then she realized her cheeks were wet with tears.

"Move."

Lifting her head, she saw the woman in the white dress, now back from the toilet, standing in front of her.

"A-ah, sorry."

Tsumugi hurriedly rose from her seat, and taking her place, the woman in the white dress slid into the space between the table and chair. Tsumugi moved to the next seat, placed the ribboned box given to her by Ayame on the table, took a handkerchief from her shoulder bag, and wiped her tears.

"How did it go?"

Hirai, who had been sitting at the counter, called out to her. At her question, tears that she thought she had wiped away began to overflow again.

"I couldn't do anything," Tsumugi answered, keeping her back turned to Hirai.

I didn't even tell her that I was sorry.

She had been obsessed over something so petty. If only she had agreed to meet Ayame when she first received her text about waiting in this café, she might have learned earlier about her illness. Then, just maybe, their final parting wouldn't have been so painful. Her petty-mindedness had stolen from her what could have been a few precious months together. The more she thought, the regret flooding over her intensified. Such remorse streamed down as unforgiving tears.

"But you did go to see her, didn't you?" Hirai said gently behind her.

"I…"

Tsumugi stared at the ribbon-tied box from Ayame, her face bent in anguish. Ayame had made her confession, her honest feelings revealed in their final moments. Faced with this unexpected admission, Tsumugi was paralyzed, unsure of what to do. She had no desire to reject Ayame but also had no idea how to respond. Probably, her hesitation had hurt Ayame even more.

"If my efforts were never going to change the inevitable present, maybe it was futile to see her at all," Tsumugi said, each word weighing her down.

"It's a possibility, but…" Hirai mused, taking a drag from her cigarette at the counter. "Your world might not seem too different, but wasn't it a heart-changing moment for her?"

"What do you mean?"

"She told you she was waiting for you, didn't she?"

Instead of answering, Tsumugi stared at the box.

"So, who do you think found happiness—the girl who never got to see you or the one who did?"

"The girl who never got to see me or one who did...?"

Hirai exhaled smoke as if to say, *You figure out the rest.*

Ayame's heart?

Upon reflection, there was a world of difference.

Ayame herself had said, "Dying without being able to express my feelings would be even more painful."

Tsumugi reached for the box and unwrapped it. Inside were chocolates that seemed to be homemade by Ayame. She looked at the card squeezed between the box and the ribbon.

"Oh..." she gasped.

The card read:

Tsumugi Ito, I like you.
Will you go out with me?
14 February 2004. Ayame Matsubara.

Tsumugi's shoulders trembled with emotion.

The date on the card was a long time before they became close friends. It predated their castle conversations and before they spoke in the samurai tongue. Ayame had not been able to express her feelings toward Tsumugi since they first met.

Finally, those feelings were…

"Ayame…"

Tsumugi's sob echoed in the café. But no one rebuked her. Kazu continued her work, and the woman in the white dress quietly read her book.

Hirai tracked the cigarette smoke with her eyes.

"Kazu, can I get another coffee?"

"And one for her, too…"

"Yes, sure."

By the time the cups of coffee Kazu served Hirai and Tsumugi were touched, the coffee had gone entirely cold.

★ ★ ★ ★ ★